Midnight in Mistletoe

BREANNA LYNN

ISBN: 978-1-955359-51-1 (paperback)

Cover Design by: Mae Harden

Edited by: Happily Editing Anns

Printed in United States of America

https://breannalynnauthor.com

Nothing good happens after midnight...or does it?

One night was all it took—no names, no strings, just a fantasy fit for a fairy tale. He was my Prince Charming for one unforgettable, toe-curling night, and I let myself believe in magic... just for a little while.

But fairy tales aren't real. Not when he shows up on my doorstep a month later. Turns out my Prince Charming is the stepbrother I've never met.

Now he's spending the holidays at The Glass Slipper, my family's bed and breakfast, here to figure out why it's failing. And judging by the way he looks at me—like I'm still the only woman in the room—he wants to pick up right where our story left off.

The spark between us is still electric. Every stolen glance is a temptation. Every forbidden touch feels like a wicked twist in a love story that was never supposed to happen.

I've always known midnight comes for every fantasy. But what if this time, my stepbrother isn't the villain in my story?

What if he's the happily ever after I never saw coming?

To everyone who ever dreamed...
Be you princess or prince,
Never stop dreaming.

Once upon a time, long ago, in a land far away...
Well, actually it wasn't that far away, although
Mistletoe Creek, Tennessee, often seems more off
the beaten path where it lies nestled against the Smoky Moun-
tain foothills. And it really wasn't so long ago. A few short
months ago, the following conversation was overheard
between Fern Myers, Fawn Carter, and Merry Andrews during
their monthly meeting. When later asked, all three women
would deny the conversation ever occurred.

"It's your deal, Fern," Merry says as she glances at the
window when a colorful leaf drifts off the oak tree just outside.

Fern scoffs and stretches her fingers before picking the
well-worn deck up off the shiny table.

"I *always* deal, Merry."

"More like always cheat," Fawn mumbles.

"Excuse me?" Fern adjusts her bifocals on the edge of her
nose.

"I find it highly suspect that every time you deal, you also
seem to win."

"If you want to deal..."

"I don't. But I do want you to play fair."

"Play fair? Just because I'm lucky doesn't mean I don't—"

"Ladies!" Merry jumps in before their argument can escalate.

It wouldn't be the first time a confrontation between the two of them had been stopped before it went beyond just words.

"I really don't feel like getting kicked out of here again by Mayor Anderson. We just got invited back. And personally, I didn't care for power walking all summer in the heat."

While the mansion of the original founder of Mistletoe Creek had been turned into a combination of public gathering spaces and city offices, the last time they'd flipped the table during a card game, Mayor Anderson had been left with no other option—he had banned all three septuagenarians for the entire summer.

"I did offer for us to play Yahtzee instead," Fawn says.

"We could always actually learn bridge instead of just telling everyone that's what we play," Merry adds.

"We've been playing Texas Hold 'Em for thirty years. Yahtzee is for when I babysit my grandkids. And if we told everyone we were playing poker instead of bridge, we'd have the entire town trying to join in our games." Fern levels a look at both of the other women until they nod.

The room is silent except for the crackle of cards as they swoosh across the table along with sighs and murmurs as each woman considers her cards.

"It's too quiet." Merry drops her cards face down.

"What do you mean?" Fern asks.

"It's been ages since we've had a wedding. Or any good gossip."

"We just went to Dawn and Jack Phillips's wedding two weekends ago. Raise ten." Fawn tosses a blue chip onto the small pile and the other two follow suit.

"It was a beautiful wedding." Merry sighs, a dreamy smile playing on her lips. "Even if Fawn fell asleep during the ceremony."

"You take that back, Merry Andrews! Or I'll tell Dawn that you didn't like the light pink of her wedding dress," Fawn fires back.

Merry's eyes narrow across the table. "You wouldn't."

Fawn crosses her arms. "Try me."

"Fine. You win. I take it back." Merry's voice is nothing more than a mumble.

Fern sighs and glances between the two of them.

"I can't believe Dawn is all grown-up and married now," Fern says, trying to redirect the conversation. "I still remember when I used to babysit her."

"Such a good girl."

"I'm just glad that she and Jack finally found each other." Merry checks her bet and turns to Fawn.

"They wouldn't have if it wasn't for us," Fawn reminds the other two.

Both other women nod in agreement.

"I thought that was never going to happen no matter how many times we kept signing Dawn up to volunteer with Jack at Parks and Wildlife." Merry rolls her eyes.

Fawn shrugs. "They finally stopped fighting it."

"It was a beautiful wedding," Fern says.

"I already said that." Merry stares at Fawn.

"Who cares? It's still true."

"We need more weddings." Fawn checks her bet and Fern deals the last card.

"No one is close to dating, let alone marriage." Fern studies her cards in her hands before lifting her shrewd gaze to the five cards on the table.

"Neither were Dawn and Jack last year and look at them

now. On their honeymoon." Merry clasps her hands together and the cards in her hand crinkle.

It wouldn't be the first deck to be lost to their lack of attention. And it definitely wouldn't be the last.

"So what are we going to do about it?" Fawn asks.

"Same thing we always do," Fern responds. "Let's see, there's Pierce and Hudson. Either of whom would be a catch."

"Don't forget Robyn or Elle. But not for either of those boys." Fawn taps her lip as she adds to the list.

"No, all four of them are ready for something special. Something spectacular. It's..." Fern's voice fades as her attention shifts back to her cards.

"It's matchmaking time," Merry says and gasps when Fawn pushes in all her chips.

"All in, ladies. Who's next?"

CHAPTER 1

Elle

I *never do this.*

"So you've told me." The deep voice filters through my blood to pulse in my core a heartbeat before his lips find the sensitive skin behind my ear.

Pleasure flows from the spot, hot and sharp, and I lean into the caress.

"Mmm. Did I say that out loud?"

It's hard to concentrate with the way his hands snake along my sides, one splayed along my stomach while the other waves the keycard in front of the lock. With a whir and a click, the door unlocks, and he walks us forward until we're in the entryway of his hotel room.

It's dark, no lights on in the room, but the curve of his lips against my neck is proof of his smile. The one I've seen several times tonight—the lopsided dimple, the flash of white teeth. It's confident. Just like its owner.

He turns me slowly until my chest is flush against his, the pressure driving the electric buzz of attraction between us that much higher.

"You did."

The words are whispered against my lips before his mouth claims mine. Our tongues connect, and the need for more flutters in my belly as the flavors of whiskey and spice overwhelm me. I deepen the kiss, tangling my tongue with his in an effort to absorb more of the intoxicating flavors, throwing all semblance of the normal me out the window.

Tonight isn't about being ordinary Elle Thompson, manager of The Glass Slipper Bed & Breakfast in Mistletoe Creek, Tennessee.

No, tonight is all about fantasy.

Somehow, the universe smiled on me, and my annual trip to Nashville for a hospitality conference coincided with the hotel's masquerade ball for Halloween. While I should have been attending a seminar on the newest technology in hotel reservation systems, I'd found a secondhand dress shop.

The ice-blue silk dress was serendipity and felt like a dream when it slithered along my skin to hug my curves as if it were made for me. I'd spent almost all my money on it and the pair of silver heels the clerk produced from a different room in the store, explaining they hadn't been marked for sale yet. A Halloween store on my way back had a discount mask on sale since most people had already purchased costumes in advance of tonight's festivities.

When I'd stepped into the ballroom tonight, I wasn't plain old Elle Thompson.

Tonight, I was Cinderella.

And the man trailing hot, open-mouthed kisses down my neck was my Prince Charming.

The heat from his touch filters through the thin material as he bunches it along my hips, dragging it up with a patience that has me ready to melt into a puddle on the floor. I dig my fingernails into the smooth material of his jacket before sliding my hands between it and the crisp white shirt underneath.

"You're sure?"

The words are murmured against my collarbone, his hands bracketing my hips while he waits for my decision.

"*Yes.*"

The word still vibrates on my lips when his tongue traces the fabric along the tops of my breasts, cool air brushing along my overheated core when the dress tugs up to my waist. Lifting one of my legs, I wrap it around his hips and align my lower body to his.

"Fuuuck," he groans and pulses his hips, his erection grinding against my center.

Fireworks flicker behind my eyes. Desperation makes my fingers clumsy as I work his suit jacket off his shoulders and start my way down the placket of buttons along his shirt. His heart thunders under my palm as I spread the shirt wide, dragging my palms along the smattering of chest hair and toned muscle.

"You're too good at that."

"Too good at what?" I manage to ask through breaths.

"Touching me."

He shakes his head, leaving my dress around my waist to tug both my hands away from their exploration of his abs. Threading his fingers with mine, he lifts until my arms are pressed against the wall, hands above my head.

"Leave these here."

Excitement zings through my blood and intensifies the ache centered both in my breasts and my core. He resumes his task of pulling my dress off, his fingers grazing along my sides, and stokes my need to almost unbearable levels. I curl my fingers into my palms, nails digging crescents into the skin as sensations buffet my body based on his touch combined with anticipation.

The dress pulls free of my breasts at last, but it tangles along the edges of the mask still in place.

Gentle fingers untangle the silk from lace, and the dress drops forgotten to the floor with a hushed whisper of fabric.

"Time to lose this," he says and lifts his hands to the mask.

"No."

He freezes with his fingers skimming my cheeks.

"No?"

Much like the pumpkin, I'm afraid the removal of the mask will break the spell.

"No." I lift my hands to his and move them back to my body.

He slides them along my hips to the small of my back and tugs me away from the wall.

"No names?" he asks.

"We already said that."

We'd agreed to it earlier during our first dance. I was Cinderella and he was Charming.

"And now you want to keep the masks on."

"Yes."

He slowly walks us to the other side of the room and next to the bed.

"I want to see you."

The gravel in his voice sends a shiver down my spine. I steel my shoulders and lean over to flick on the bedside light, emboldened by the mask and assumed identity.

"Look your fill, Charming."

I step back and fist my hands on my hips while dark eyes work their way from the crown of my head to the tips of my toes still encased in the silver heels. The moment drags on for one breath, then two, before he lunges forward and fists his hands in my hair.

"I don't remember Cinderella being this sexy when I was a kid." The words are barely out before his mouth locks to mine.

He wraps one arm around my waist, spinning us until my

back is to the bed. I hiss at the coolness of the linen beneath my back while he settles into the cradle of my thighs. His hands reach under, finding the catch on my strapless bra and freeing it with one twist of his fingers before he pulls the fabric away from my body.

My nipples pebble in the cool air and tighten further with the scrutiny of his heated gaze.

"This isn't a fairy tale," I tell him.

He lifts his gaze to mine.

"It's a fantasy," I clarify.

Fairy tales involve happily ever after. I'd rather have an orgasm or two.

"Fantasy, huh?"

One side of his lips quirks, and that kissable dimple goes on display.

"Ye—ohhh."

Without warning, he drops his head and sucks one of my nipples into his mouth. My fingers fly to his hair, holding him in place as I press myself against him.

"More," I beg.

His teeth nip sharply before he releases my breast with a pop.

"What's this?"

My eyes flutter open. He lifts the delicate silver chain with the ring that's been nestled between my breasts all night.

Reality pushes at the bubble of pleasure I've created, and I swallow thickly before lifting the chain from his fingers and tugging the necklace off to lay it on the nightstand.

I shift my arm back along my body until my fingers wrap around my other nipple. I pinch roughly, and my legs tighten around his waist.

"What are you doing?"

His dick pulses against my inner thigh, and I repeat the motion and cry out as my eyelids drift closed.

"What does it look like?" My voice is husky as the pleasure rebuilds and drives out the reality threatening to intrude.

"My job."

Before I can repeat the caress for the third time, he bats my fingers away and sinks his teeth roughly into the hardened tip. The necklace with my mother's wedding ring is forgotten.

"You're wearing too many clothes," I complain when my hands encounter the starched collar of his dress shirt.

"Easily remedied."

He lifts himself from the bed and shrugs out of the shirt. The dim light highlights the muscles that roll and dip along his arms, and he drags one hand down his chest to rest at his belt. I shift until I can drag my thong down my legs and watch his eyes darken further behind the black mask he wears. He palms himself through his pants before frantically working the button and zipper.

I spread my legs and trace one finger along my inner thigh.

"Don't you fucking dare."

"What?" I ask.

"The only one who touches that pussy tonight will be me." A command exists in his voice that hasn't been there before.

"Or what?" I slide my finger closer and he growls.

He yanks his wallet out of his pants pocket and tosses the condom he retrieves on the bed. He tosses the wallet behind him and tugs pants and boxers down to kick them free while his dick points in my direction.

"Or else."

I smile, enjoying the fire I can freely play with tonight. I drag my finger another inch closer.

"Or else what?"

His eyes flash, and he leans down to grab the belt from the loop on his pants. His erection bobs as he moves closer and grabs both my wrists in one hand. Wrapping the leather around several times, he tugs it through the buckle and checks his handiwork before lifting my now joined hands above my head. I tug at the restraint, and a slight trace of fear edges along the rest of the desire when it doesn't move.

Who am I kidding? I've known this man a few hours. What if—

"It's only for a minute," he assures me, and my eyes clash with his.

"How..."

"You've only known me for a night, Cinderella, but I'm no beast. This is all fun. It's still your fantasy, sweets. But when you tease me, expect consequences."

"C-consequences?" I swallow and try to find the confident woman from a few moments ago.

"Yes."

He sits on the side of the bed and runs his hand along my outer leg from the ankle strap of my shoes to just above my knee. It's a light caress, but the charge still exists. My thighs relax, and I part my legs.

"What kinds of consequences?"

He smirks and repeats the gentle caress on the inside of my leg but trails his fingers higher, still stopping short where the ache is starting to build again.

I fidget and part my legs farther, waiting for him to respond.

"Charming?" I ask when he only continues to repeat the caress until I'm about to go crazy.

He turns and kneels at my feet before he pushes one leg up and back followed by the other. His gaze zeroes in between my legs, and I swear he has some sort of heat vision the way my pussy warms under the attention.

"These kinds of consequences."

He shifts so fast, I don't fully understand what he says until he licks along my pussy from back to front and swirls his tongue around my clit. I almost process one sensation when he changes up what he's doing and pleasure drives every other thought from my mind. But like some orgasm-sensing oracle, he stops and changes only when I'm on the verge of coming.

"Please," I beg and tug at the belt still wrapped around my wrists.

I can't touch him, can't touch myself, and it ratchets the ache up to a whole new spectrum. Tongue still buried in my pussy, he tugs on the belt and the restraint falls free. My hands fist in the sheets before they find purchase in his hair. I press him closer while I lift my hips. The orgasm continues to build. Layer after layer of pleasure until I'm facing a wall of bright light, hurtling toward an orgasm more powerful than any I've ever experienced before. It's terrifying. It's incredible. It's a mix of the two where I can't tell where one sensation begins and the other ends.

"Don't stop," I whimper.

He grunts and slides one finger in before curling it upward.

The light shatters around me. I am the light. I am nothing but the pleasure coursing through my body in wave after powerful wave. My hips buck against him and he holds me in place, wringing every drop of pleasure from the orgasm until I drift back to earth in boneless bliss. I'm only vaguely aware of the crinkle of foil before the heat of him moves up, his arms on either side of my head while his lips find mine in a kiss so carnal it burns itself vividly into my brain.

My legs wrap around his hips as he thrusts forward to the hilt. Aftershocks of pleasure shoot along my legs, and my thighs tighten involuntarily.

His retreat and return is a rhythm my body tunes itself to, and I meet his next thrust with one of my own, my body demanding I do it again and again until another orgasm shimmers at the edges. He flexes his fingers into my ass, lifting me faster as his tempo increases. My grip slides along his sweat-slickened shoulders and finds purchase on his biceps as his body pushes mine closer to the edge.

"Are you close?" he grits out.

My pussy tightens as pleasure licks along my toes, the calm before the full storm right on top of the two of us now.

"I—"

It's the only word I can manage between breaths.

In another quick move, he retreats completely, flipping me over before thrusting back inside with the same rhythm as before. One hand grips my hip while the other holds my neck. He hits deeper this way, the orgasm intensifying as it crashes down and drowns me in a pleasure echoed by his own groan of release and sets off a third I didn't know existed. Pleasure rockets through me, my only tether the man who works us both through the release before he collapses against my shoulder.

"Holy shit." His breath tightens my nipple and he groans. "Do it again."

"Do what?"

"Tighten that sweet pussy for me again."

When my nipple tightened, my pussy must have too. I tighten my muscles and hold the contraction longer before releasing.

"That?"

"Mmm."

His lips find my shoulder before he lifts himself off me and wanders to the bathroom to dispose of the condom.

"What are you doing?" he asks, washcloth in hand when he returns.

"You ask that question a lot," I tell him and reach for my dress again.

"I wouldn't have to if I knew what you were doing."

His mask is askew, but the heat of his gaze is still palpable between us.

"Well, we..." I gesture between the two of us.

He closes the distance and tugs the dress from my hands to drop it to the floor again.

"We had sex. Great sex. Which we can have more of. If you stay."

"But—"

This isn't my first one-night stand. Usually once the itch is scratched, we go our separate ways.

So why does it feel like the itch needs to be scratched again?

"Stay." His lips coast along mine until his tongue teases the edge to request entry.

Who could say no to that?

Light peeks through the curtains when I wake up hours later. I'm naked.

Completely.

My fingers brush bare skin instead of the mask that was in place when I fell asleep, and panic sets in. Where is it?

My brain is foggy with the lack of sleep—Charming was definitely true to his word that we could have more great sex— and my muscles ache deliciously. But the mask being gone is the slap back to reality I need.

Cinderella is gone and it's time to be Elle Thompson again.

Easing my way from the bed, I tiptoe to my dress and slide the wrinkled fabric over my head. Good thing I only have a few floors for a walk of shame. Searching for my bra, I see it poking out from under Charming's prone form but can't risk getting it back. His dress shirt is crumpled next to the foot of the bed and I lift it, shaking it gently and lifting it to my nose.

Sandalwood and lavender. Masculine spice.

Quit mooning over his shirt and get out of here!

Wrapping the shirt around me, I don't bother to button it and reach down for my shoes.

What else? My eyes begin to scan the room, and the man face down on the bed—his mask is gone too—murmurs and reaches where I was just lying.

"Sweets?" he murmurs.

It's my cue to leave.

Tiptoeing to the door, I thank the high-end hotel for no squeaky hinges—a reminder to order some WD-40 when I go home—and close the door as quietly as I can behind me. At this time of morning, the hotel hallway is vacant, but I'd rather not encounter anyone in the elevator who might be leaving early.

The stairwell is to my left, and I take the three flights to my floor and grab the keycard from the small purse I'd dropped in Charming's room as soon as we walked in. I don't breathe until the door is closed behind me and I lean against it.

The conference is over and so is Halloween.

"Midnight has come and gone, Cinderella. Time to go home."

CHAPTER 2

Elle

The phantom smells of lavender and sandalwood tickle my nose moments before the alarm shrilly interrupts my memories of my fantasy night with Charming—not that they aren't always waiting to be called on when I want them. My BOB has gotten more of a workout in the last month than it has in the year I've owned it. My fingers twitch and demand that I reach for the drawer, but I stop myself.

Barely.

"No time today," I mumble and reach for my phone instead to shut off the alarm.

3:45 a.m.

"Run a bed and breakfast, they said. It'll be fun, they said."

Tossing back the covers, I sit up on the edge of the bed and scrub my hands down my face. It *was* fun. I remember when my parents ran the B&B and helping them after school and on the weekends. Mom would wake up early to make the pastries for breakfast, and Dad would sit in the kitchen and keep her company.

The B&B is the epicenter of town events, opening its doors for open houses for all the major holidays, like today—Thanksgiving. While we are closed for guests in the traditional sense, we will host the open house for town residents to pop in and have breakfast or hors d'oeuvres and drinks later before they all head home for their own dinners. Then I will have to put dinner out for my stepmother, Trudy, my stepsister, Alysa, and according to my stepmother, her son, Channing, is coming for the holidays and will be here in time for dinner.

Oh goody. Another spoiled Kingsley child. As if my step-sister and stepmother weren't enough to handle. Not that I know Channing Kingsley from Adam. Despite my dad being married to my stepmother for five years before he passed away three years ago, I've never met him.

A breeze rattles against the window and shakes me from my thoughts.

"Okay, okay, I'm up." I stand and stretch my arms over my head.

The cold floorboards creak with each step, and I wince and think about laying a carpet down for the umpteenth time, but I hate to cover up the original floors—even if it is the attic. I've long since given up my room to try to generate more revenue for the B&B, but despite being booked at near capacity most of the year, it doesn't seem to make a chink in the debt my stepmother and stepsister rack up.

Tossing on my Volunteers hoodie that has seen better days, I make my way quietly downstairs and only turn on the lights when I reach the kitchen. I blink against the sudden brightness and wait to walk over to the coffeemaker when I've adjusted to the light.

With the twist of the knob on the fancy coffeemaker I consider one of my small indulgences, I pull out the ingredients I prepped the night before—the cinnamon roll dough is first to be shaped and set aside as I wait for the oven to preheat, followed by the chocolate chip scones. The oven beeps, and I move the rolls to the rack and keep my assembly line going with the lemon blueberry breakfast cake. I've made the cake so many times, I no longer need a recipe in front of me, but like every other pastry I make, nothing is as good as when Mom made it.

"What would today be like if you were still here?" I ask.

Would I be married? Still live in Mistletoe Creek? Have a kid or two? Most of my friends—at least the ones I still manage to connect with—are married with a few kids now that we are entering our thirties. I had been on a similar track, engaged when my stepmother called to tell me Dad had been in a car accident. That there wasn't any more money for me to stay in Knoxville and I needed to come home.

At twenty-seven, I'd almost been done with my degree after taking a few years off when Mom got sick. Even after Mom passed away, I didn't want to leave Dad alone, only moving out once Trudy and Alysa moved in and I felt like they could take care of him. So at twenty-three, when most people were graduating, I'd started my degree again. It was slow going since I only did school part time, splitting my time as much as I could between Knoxville and home, still worried about Dad. But when Trudy called, I had come home, finishing my degree online class by class and accepting the fact that my fiancé Carter broke our engagement because I worked all the time and lived an hour away. Even when I was off, my schedule took its toll—getting up at four in the morning meant bedtime came early.

The lightening of the sky distracts me from the bacon and egg breakfast tarts I'm putting together, and I straighten and stretch.

I haven't thought about Carter in a long time—even before my night with Charming. Him, I couldn't get off my mind. I hadn't had that issue the other two times I'd had one-night stands when I'd been in Nashville. The only time away I got from the B&B was the hospitality conference hosted for one weekend a year.

But this year with Halloween and the masquerade ball, it had been different. It had been...my hands freeze as I try to find the right word.

Fantasy.

That night with him had been a once-in-a-lifetime dream.

I was never going to see him again. I had no idea why he was even at the hotel, let alone expect him to go next year. If I got to go. The way reservations were dropping off, I doubted the B&B would still be running by next year. It was like losing my parents all over again.

I blink the moisture from my eyes and take a deep breath.

I'm not going to let that happen.

I can't.

I just need to figure out how.

My phone vibrates across the counter as the timer goes off for the cinnamon rolls, and I tuck the phone between my neck and shoulder and reach for my oven mitts.

"You're up early," I say by way of greeting.

"Early? I haven't been to bed yet."

Posey Andrews has been my best friend since we started kindergarten. But she moved to Charlotte and works for a marketing firm for their tourism industry. As my only friend who isn't married with children, Posey—whose real name is Persephone—never grew out of her party days in college.

"I thought you were coming home for Thanksgiving?"

"Chill, drama queen. I'm at the airport."

"Good."

I haven't seen Posey since earlier this year when she came for our friend Dawn's wedding. I was looking forward to seeing her this weekend and maybe grabbing lunch if I could break away for a little while.

Shouldn't be hard when the only guest was stepfamily.

"Ready to have some fun this weekend?"

I laugh.

"You do realize you're heading to Mistletoe Creek at the holidays, right? The only thing going on is holiday related."

"So we'll stop at The Woodsman and grab dinner, smuggle out some of their famous peppermint liquor, and mix it with a thermos of hot chocolate to drink in the town square."

"Girl, the last time we did that we ended up drunk in my parents' kitchen at one in the morning."

And neither of them had been pleased since they had to get up a few hours later.

Posey snorts.

"Yeah, something tells me the stepmonster would *love* that."

I shudder and adjust the phone before I pop the tray of scones in the oven.

"Yeah, I'd rather avoid that interaction if I can."

"Is her son still coming for Thanksgiving?"

"As far as I know."

"Well, I land in Knoxville around two. You're still hosting the Thanksgiving Open House?"

"Yep, breakfast is almost ready now."

"I'll swing by before I hit up Mom and Dad's. See if you need rescuing from the troll."

A loud announcement echoes behind her and she sighs.

"Everything okay?" I ask.

"Just a delay, but it only shortens my layover in Dallas."

"Where are you?"

"The airport."

"Smart-ass," I tell her. "Which airport?"

Last time I had talked to her, she was on her way to a business trip.

"LAX. And of course I have the layover in Dallas before I fly to Knoxville."

"Do you get to stay for a while?"

"For a few days at least. But when I leave, I have to go to Atlanta and then Charlotte. Why?"

"Nothing nonstop?"

"It was all sold out by the time I remembered to book my ticket."

"When did you book your ticket?" I ask even though something tells me I already know the answer.

"Last week."

"Persephone!"

"I know."

"You're lucky you got *any* ticket."

"That's what Mom said too."

"When did she tell you that?"

"Last week when she called to remind me to buy the ticket."

I laugh.

"She knows you pretty well."

"Yep."

The timer goes off on the oven again, and the intercom alarms at the same time.

"Ugh. I have to go. Can't wait to see you tonight!" I tell her as the alarm on the intercom rings again.

"Me neither!"

I hang up and my cell phone rings again immediately. This time I roll my eyes and answer while also pulling the scones out.

"Elle, I've been buzzing for the last fifteen minutes."

My stepmother's voice grates through the phone like nails on a chalkboard.

I keep my comment on her inability to tell time to myself.

"I'm so sorry, Trudy. I've been working on finishing breakfast."

"Is it done now?"

"Almost."

"I want coffee."

I bite my tongue to keep the snark out of my voice as best I can.

"Yes, ma'am."

I move to the cabinet for her coffee mug.

"From Mistletoe Café."

"Trudy, they're not open today."

"Well, why the hell not?"

"It's a holiday," I remind her.

Maybe she forgot since every day is a holiday for her. She hasn't lifted a finger to work since my dad passed away.

"Why does that matter? If I still lived in Nashville I could order what I wanted even if it was a holiday."

You don't live in Nashville anymore. And she hasn't for the better part of a decade. But I don't dare say that out loud.

"I can make you a coffee," I offer through gritted teeth.

Her sigh is more long-suffering than it should be.

"Fine."

"I'll have it up to you in just a minute."

"I want a cinnamon roll too."

Of course she does.

"Anything else?"

"No."

The phone beeps in my ear, and my fingers tighten around the rectangle as I contemplate tossing it across the room. But it isn't what I'm annoyed with. Instead I set it down on the counter and move to the coffeemaker to fix her coffee.

The intercom buzzes again and I rush to the button.

"Did you need something else, Trudy?"

"I want coffee." My stepsister's voice cracks through the intercom.

Would a "please" kill either her or my stepmother?

Honestly, it probably would.

But arguing takes more time than I have today.

"I'll bring one up when I bring up Trudy's."

"You better."

Rolling my eyes, I grab another mug and brew her coffee next. The breakfast trays are where they've been since my parents opened The Glass Slipper the year before I was born—the cabinet above the refrigerator. The next few minutes are a choreography of dishing up two cinnamon rolls since even though she didn't ask for one yet, Alysa will demand one as soon as I go upstairs, setting the plates and coffee on the tray, and snagging the scones from the oven before I put in the lemon blueberry cake.

I've lifted heavier trays before so this one is easy to lift, but just as quickly I have to put it down when the doorbell rings.

"Who on earth would be here this early?"

I wipe my hands on the front of my Volunteers hoodie and leave the kitchen to go to the front door.

"Can I help—"

Every other word leaves my brain in a rush of dopamine and serotonin at the perfect male specimen standing on my front porch. A pair of aviators are perched on his nose, and his dark hair is styled in a way that gives the appearance of messy but is anything but. If it's possible to stand with swagger, whoever this is has it down pat.

"Good morning. Channing Kingsley."

He pulls off his sunglasses, and dark eyes move from my messy bun down the front of my sweatshirt and yoga pants to my Uggs, as a trail of heat follows in their wake. When his eyes meet mine again, he smiles, a dimple bracketing one side of his mouth highlighted by the layer of scruff covering his cheeks.

Lopsided smile.

Dark eyes.

I suck in a breath, notes of sandalwood and lavender reaching out to smack me in the olfactory sense.

Holy. Shit.

Charming is in my house.

No, not Charming.

My stepbrother. Channing Kingsley.

Holy. Fucking. Shit.

I had sex.

Mind-blowing, unforgettable sex.

With my stepbrother.

Channing

The blonde doesn't take my outstretched hand, her big, brown eyes getting wider the longer she stares at me. I glance down to make sure I haven't spilled something down the front of me or left my fly down—either is a possibility given how tired I am after the long flight back from Australia in time to visit my mother and sister for the holidays. Nothing is amiss, my navy sweater pristine and my zipper perfectly in place.

Maybe I should have stayed longer at the hotel. Tried to get more sleep instead of leaving before dawn to come here. But sleep was hard to come by at the hotel I helped redesign a little over two years ago. It might have been familiar, but my thoughts were occupied elsewhere.

On her.

Cinderella.

The odds of seeing her again at the hotel—of recognizing her without her costume—were slim to none. I'd woken that morning last month to the click of the door latch, my foggy mind taking several precious moments to process what had happened and that she was gone.

27

By the time I hit the hallway half-naked, there was no sign of her. The whole experience could almost be chalked up to a dream, except for the necklace on the floor between the nightstand and bed that caught the light from the curtains when I opened them. The delicate diamond on the thin chain was my only souvenir that was even now tucked into the luggage in the back of my rental.

Mother had asked me to stay for the holidays and give her some advice on whether the bed and breakfast should be sold in light of the decrease in reservations. If the mute in front of me was any indication, I had my work cut out for me.

"And you are?" I ask, arching a brow and withdrawing my hand to tuck it into my pocket.

"Y-y-you're Channing?"

A pretty flush fills her cheeks, and my dick kicks to life in my pants. I attempt to ignore the zing of attraction and focus on the fact that I have no idea who she is. Someone Mother hired for the cooking based on the streaks of food down a faded sweatshirt. I hoped her culinary skills were better than her social ones.

Who needs to talk? Those lips are made more for kissing than speaking. Or even better wrapped around your dick.

My attention drifts to the pale-pink cupid's bow that's slightly parted as she pulls in a breath. Does she taste as sweet as she looks? Even as disheveled as she is, I can't completely ignore the pull she seems to have on me.

"Yes, I am. But the question of the moment is who are you?" I repeat, a little slower.

She opens her mouth, but it's Mother's voice that echoes down the stairs.

"Why on earth are you standing in the open door... Channing! I wasn't expecting you until later."

She rushes down the remainder of the stairs and bumps the blonde out of the way to wrap me in a hug of powerful perfume. The thickness of the cloud is overpowering at this time of morning, and it takes everything in me to return the hug before I can lean up for fresh air. By the time I can tactfully extricate myself from Mother's grip, the blonde is long gone.

"Come in, come in," Mother says, yanking me into the house and slamming the door with a dramatic shiver. "I hope you weren't out in that cold too long."

That cold is somewhere between forty and fifty degrees, and I'd been too preoccupied with the woman who greeted me to notice the temperature.

I wave away her concern. "It's not too bad. I didn't realize you hired a cook."

Mother leads the way to a sitting room and I follow.

"Cook?" She turns, the confusion clear on her face. "Elle?"

"That's Elle?" I ask.

Based on Mother's description, I hadn't expected to have the door opened this morning by my stepsister. Mother was constantly complaining about how little Elle did around the bed and breakfast.

"Of course that's her. Who else would answer the door?"

"I thought you said you couldn't find any help with this place."

The pieces are starting to click together, and her wide-eyed look of innocence is confirmation.

"No, dear, I said I couldn't find *good* help. Not in this little hovel of a small town."

Based on my drive through the picturesque little town, I wouldn't quite describe Mistletoe Creek as a hovel. It is... charming.

"Am I missing something? The town is quaint, but—"

"Quaint?" Her voice raises an octave and I hide my wince. "It's nothing more than a viper's nest of greedy people. You'll see them all today when they swarm this place like locusts—"

Lifting my hand, I attempt to stem her tirade.

"You would know this place better than I would, Mother."

She sniffs. "Yes, I would."

We sit in awkward silence for several ticks of the grandfather clock from the entryway. Being as nomadic as I've been for the last fourteen years, I had forgotten Mother's opinionated view of the world and her displeasure when she wasn't agreed with.

"I need coffee." She stands and is almost to the doorway by the time I speak.

"Maybe you can show me where I'm staying while I'm here and we can both grab some?"

She sighs and nods. "Fine. Come on."

The floral wallpaper in the stairwell is faded, the forest-green carpet clean, but from a different time as well. But the wooden banister is clean, polished to a shine, and smooth beneath my fingertips. The bones of this place are good, but it definitely needs a face lift.

Mother stops at the top of the stairs, and Alysa's voice is clear even though none of the doors in the hallway are open.

"I don't care if they're closed. I don't want this shit."

There's a crash and Blondie—Elle—comes out of the last door on the right. Unlike the pretty pink from earlier, her cheeks redden when she sees the two of us. Embarrassment? Anger? A combination of the two.

"Elle, show Channing to Room 2. I'm going to get coffee."

She's gone as soon as the words are out of her mouth, walking back down the stairs as if getting her caffeine is the number one priority. Granted, some mornings I can definitely agree, but I expected her to be somewhat happier to see me than she is.

"It's just right here," Elle murmurs and moves to the door across from where she just left.

With a flick of her wrist, she twists the knob and motions me inside.

"You leave the doors unlocked?"

She bristles.

"Only when we don't have any guests. It's easier for cleaning and all the in and out I do to prepare rooms."

"Sorry, I didn't mean to sound judgmental. It was only a question." I lift a hand to her shoulder, and my fingers sizzle with the electric current that travels at the innocent touch.

What the fuck was that?

Her quick intake of breath is proof she felt it too. It isn't jet lag then. And it's not one-sided.

It is, however, awfully damn inconvenient.

She is my stepsister. Despite the fact that I've never met her until today, I shouldn't be attracted to her. It takes more effort than I care to admit to remove my hand from her arm and shift my attention to the room in front of us. It looks more modern than the rest of what I've seen, but still could use some modernization. Thankfully, the lacy pink frills I was dreading aren't present anywhere, and I breathe a sigh of relief at the deep blues and more masculine tone of the room.

"What did my sister break?" I ask quietly.

I may have released the physical connection, but something else tethers me to share the doorway with her.

"A teacup."

She sinks her teeth into her trembling lower lip, and the desire to lift my hand and use my fingers to release the flesh from its pearly prison is strong enough that I clench them into fists instead.

What the hell is wrong with you?

"An important one," I say.

It's not a question. Not with her reaction, but she still nods.

"It was my mother's."

"Was?" I rack my brain, sifting through eight years of memories for any mention Mother would have made of her late husband's first wife.

"She passed away."

Fuck. This is great conversation, especially for a holiday.

"I'm so sorry."

I lift my hand again—an automatic response meant to comfort—but second-guess my decision given my first experience with the electric current that charged through me with touching her.

She shrugs, but it's more a staged response than anything I've experienced from her thus far.

"It was a long time ago."

"It doesn't mean I'm not still sorry. I lost my dad twenty years ago."

Deep-brown eyes the color of hot chocolate meet mine, and her fingers graze my hand.

"I'm sorry."

I can't move, can't look away, and draw a deep breath, filling my lungs with the scents of vanilla and cream. Dark eyes hold a warmth that I want to fall into like wrapping up in a warm blanket on a crisp fall morning.

The reaction is so familiar, but how can it be?

"It feels like we've met before," I murmur. "Have we?"

Something flickers in her eyes, but before I can place it, she shakes her head.

"How can we? You've been all over the world. I've never been outside Tennessee."

"I just...this is going to sound weird, but it feels like I've known you forever."

The soft line of her jaw is tempting me to trace it with my finger. Or at least to start with.

Fuck. I've never reacted this way to a woman.

What about Cinderella?

That was different. *She* was different. I hadn't been able to *not* go up and introduce myself. And then I couldn't tear myself away.

"Did you need anything else?"

To know if you taste as sweet as you look.

She's my fucking stepsister. Not some woman I met on a trip to scratch an itch with.

I swallow thickly and clear my throat when it sticks partway down.

"No."

My voice squeaks like an eleven-year-old boy's and I want to groan. Elle studies me quizzically before she slowly nods.

"If you do, I'll be in the kitchen."

"Mother said something about an event?"

She nods, and a strand of blonde hair waves along her cheek.

"It's our annual Thanksgiving open house. We start with breakfast and coffee and end with drinks and hors d'oeuvres later today."

"Do you need any help?"

She shakes her head, and for the first time, I'm graced with an impish smile. One I like very much.

"No offense, but you look like you're about to fall over. I don't know how much help you'll be if you pass out in my kitchen."

"None taken—this time. My trip from Australia took longer than expected thanks to some mechanical issues."

"Australia?" Those gorgeous eyes widen again.

"Yeah." My word ends on a yawn, and my arms itch to stretch up, but I hold them still.

"How about a nap?" She motions to the bed.

"You're probably right. I didn't sleep well last night."

"Probably not if you were in a cramped plane seat."

"Oh, I flew in yesterday afternoon. I ended up staying at the Royal Mill."

"The Royal Mill?" All the color drains from her face.

"Yeah. Do you know it? They host a hospitality conference every year. I was there about a month ago too and was a speaker."

"I...was there," she admits reluctantly.

"You were? That must be why you look so familiar. You must have sat in my seminar."

"Not that I know of. I would have remembered seeing my stepbrother give a speech. I don't even remember seeing your name."

"I was a last-minute substitution when one of the original presenters was sick."

"W-what was your topic?" she asks.

"Modernizing the boutique hotel in a holistic approach. It's all about taking these types of hotels, like the bed and breakfast, and making them more modern and more appealable to the Airbnb and VRBO crowd."

"Oh."

"Elle, are you all right?"

Lifting my hand, I cup her elbow, but she shakes off the touch almost immediately.

"I am. Sorry, just thinking about what I still have to do today. If you'll excuse me."

"Oh, of course. Would you mind telling my mother I'm going to lie down for a little bit?"

She nods, mute once again as she retreats from the room.

"Oh, and Elle?"

I wait until her gaze clashes with mine.

"Yeah?"

"It's nice meeting you finally."

"Nice to meet you too."

I close the door behind her and kick off my shoes before lying down on the soft bed. Elle's vanilla and cream smells have infused themselves in the room, and I take another deep breath. But when I close my eyes, for the first time in a month, the vision of the woman behind my eyelids isn't Cinderella.

It's Elle.

Channing

The ring of my phone drags me from a dreamless sleep. It stops before my clumsy fingers can grip the smooth surface but starts immediately again. This time, I'm more successful and connect the call before bringing the device to my ear.

"'Lo?"

"Fuck you, you lazy ass. Quit sleeping the day away and get some work done." My best friend's voice is loud in my ear, and I pull the phone an inch away.

"Asshole. It's a holiday. And I only landed yesterday from Australia," I remind him.

Besides being my best friend, Hayden Underwood is my business partner. And while I flew nearly twenty-four hours to Tennessee, Hayden flew the three or so hours to Fiji to start prepping for the next job.

"Did you forget that your flight was significantly shorter than mine and you at least got to stay in the same day of the week?" I growl.

"Grumpy," he says with a laugh, and I can easily conjure the image of me strangling him.

I don't dignify his comment with a response.

"Aww, c'mon, Chan. I'm only on my first cup of coffee here and the sun is barely up. I feel your pain."

"The fuck you do. What do you want?"

Sitting up, I use my free hand to rub the grit of sleep from my eyes.

"Just wanted you to know I met with the owner of Grand Paradise."

"What do you think?"

He snorts.

"The pictures don't do it justice. The 'Grand Paradise Hotel' had its grandeur twenty years ago."

"The pictures were bad enough," I groan. "How did the meeting with the owner go?"

"It went...okay."

"Only okay?"

"You know I don't usually do these meetings."

"Yes, but you also know how to string two sentences together like an adult."

"I did fine!"

"So what happened?" I ask.

"The owner mentioned a couple of meetings with developers from the bigwig resort next door. They want to purchase the property."

"For what?"

I sit up straighter. This job was the opening we needed for more tropical destinations. No way did I want to give that up when we'd worked for almost fifteen years to get it.

"He didn't say."

"More than likely they didn't tell him. They probably want to rip the entire building down and use it for parking. Or staff housing."

"It's happened before."

"Did you explain that with what our plans are, we can

Channing

The ring of my phone drags me from a dreamless sleep. It stops before my clumsy fingers can grip the smooth surface but starts immediately again. This time, I'm more successful and connect the call before bringing the device to my ear.

"'Lo?"

"Fuck you, you lazy ass. Quit sleeping the day away and get some work done." My best friend's voice is loud in my ear, and I pull the phone an inch away.

"Asshole. It's a holiday. And I only landed yesterday from Australia," I remind him.

Besides being my best friend, Hayden Underwood is my business partner. And while I flew nearly twenty-four hours to Tennessee, Hayden flew the three or so hours to Fiji to start prepping for the next job.

"Did you forget that your flight was significantly shorter than mine and you at least got to stay in the same day of the week?" I growl.

"Grumpy," he says with a laugh, and I can easily conjure the image of me strangling him.

I don't dignify his comment with a response.

"Aww, c'mon, Chan. I'm only on my first cup of coffee here and the sun is barely up. I feel your pain."

"The fuck you do. What do you want?"

Sitting up, I use my free hand to rub the grit of sleep from my eyes.

"Just wanted you to know I met with the owner of Grand Paradise."

"What do you think?"

He snorts.

"The pictures don't do it justice. The 'Grand Paradise Hotel' had its grandeur twenty years ago."

"The pictures were bad enough," I groan. "How did the meeting with the owner go?"

"It went...okay."

"Only okay?"

"You know I don't usually do these meetings."

"Yes, but you also know how to string two sentences together like an adult."

"I did fine!"

"So what happened?" I ask.

"The owner mentioned a couple of meetings with developers from the bigwig resort next door. They want to purchase the property."

"For what?"

I sit up straighter. This job was the opening we needed for more tropical destinations. No way did I want to give that up when we'd worked for almost fifteen years to get it.

"He didn't say."

"More than likely they didn't tell him. They probably want to rip the entire building down and use it for parking. Or staff housing."

"It's happened before."

"Did you explain that with what our plans are, we can

who she was, take her out without the costume. Maybe even have more life-altering sex. But happily ever after?

"Maybe."

I don't mention the front desk clerk at the Royal Mill who was bewildered by my line of questioning that started with whether she knew Cinderella or if anyone had called looking for a missing necklace.

No, she did not, and she couldn't disclose if anyone had or hadn't.

"Stranger things have happened," he says.

"It was a chance encounter. But that's it."

"So you're done?"

"Yes."

The word sticks in my throat. I'd never felt the way I did before that night. And hadn't had a glimmer of attraction to anyone else since.

Except Elle.

She's your stepsister. Off-limits!

Off-limits or not, something still drew me to her.

"I have to go."

I hang up on a sputtering Hayden and silence my phone so I can ignore the text spamming about to start.

I've spent enough of the day in this room.

It's time to go get to know my stepsister.

The hum of voices reaches me at the top of the stairs.

How many people are here?

Elle had said that the bed and breakfast hosted an open house all day on Thanksgiving, but I knew from Mother that there were no bookings for the holiday. Money was going out to put on this party, and nothing was coming in to offset it.

Between hemorrhaging money like this and the decor that

looked like it fit more in the 1990s, no wonder she had called me to identify the potential for a sale. It's not like either she or my sister were businesswomen—the bed and breakfast had belonged to my stepfather until he passed and bequeathed the place to Mother.

But why her and not his daughter?

She wasn't a businesswoman. Better on menial tasks than on keeping the bed and breakfast running.

As if conjured, she walks past the bottom of the stairs, a tray of something that looks delicious in her hand. Gone is the sloppily tossed-up hair and stained sweatshirt. Instead, soft waves now cascade down her back, set off by the baby-pink sweater and jeans that hug her curves with mouthwatering results. My fingers itch to test the softness of the material. Is her skin even softer beneath?

What the fuck is wrong with you? She's your stepsister!

My dick doesn't seem to realize the distinction and presses against the zipper of my jeans.

Elle disappears through the doorway, bumping into my sister who is engrossed in the contents of her phone on the way out.

"Watch it," she snarls.

Elle doesn't respond and Alysa turns toward the stairs, glancing up as she begins the ascent.

"Channing? You're here already?" Excitement creates a shrill element to her voice and I wince.

She rushes up the stairs, launching herself at me. I band one arm around her waist.

"Hi, Lys, yeah. I headed here early to surprise you and Mom." I lower her feet to the floor and she steps back.

"And you're staying through Christmas?"

"That's the plan."

"The plan?" Her nose wrinkles and her excitement dims.

"Unless Hayden needs me for the current job we're trying to pitch."

"But you promised!" She stamps her foot like a three-year-old throwing a tantrum instead of a twenty-five-year-old woman.

"Lys, I'll do what I can. Hopefully Hayden doesn't need me after all."

Reaching out, I squeeze her shoulder, but I'm more than a little taken aback by my baby sister's change in behavior. Maybe she's not the same Alysa I remember. Then again, she's not thirteen anymore.

"You'd think your job was more important than we are."

"Lys—"

She stalks past me and into her room, slamming the door behind her. The sound echoes in the hallway and surrounds me with a thud.

A headache is forming behind my eyes, and I'm half tempted to go back to my room and go back to bed. Or knock on Alysa's door and figure out what I did to deserve the level of attitude I just got.

"I miss tween Alysa who didn't give me this much attitude," I mumble and turn back toward the stairs.

The sitting room is warm and cheery once I make my way to it, and several pockets of people are all engaged in conversation. Or at least until I come into the room. It should be funny. It would be if I wasn't the cause for everyone to stare quietly at my entrance as if I'm lit by some spotlight that screams "New Person."

I clear my throat and nod.

Mother is the first to start her conversation back up with two older-looking gentlemen and a younger couple, but three elderly women with blue hair and shrewd gazes continue to stare at me even after I cross the room to where Elle is rearranging various appetizers on a table set up by the picture window.

"What's all this?" I ask and reach past her to snag a neatly sliced carrot.

Heat radiates along her arm, electricity arcing between the two of us where my fingers almost graze the material.

"We have a charcuterie board, baked brie, a veggie tray, and some olives. I'll be bringing out the homemade biscuits and preserves in a bit, or if you'd like something else, there are still some leftover scones and stuff from the breakfast options..." Her fingers lift and flutter against the neckline of her sweater before she drops them awkwardly.

She turns, intent on retreating away from our conversation, but she's the only one I want to talk to.

"Wait."

She stiffens at the hand I lay on her arm and I remove it. She's fidgety, her eyes wandering the room.

"Why?"

My tongue is thick in my mouth, and it's as if I'm fourteen years old again trying to talk to a pretty girl while my words are wrapped like cotton in my mouth.

"I...we should get to know each other. I don't know anything about you other than you're Mark's daughter."

Again she stiffens and I kick myself.

Yeah, great idea, Kingsley. Bring up her dead dad on a holiday. Maybe you want to talk about her mother too and remind her that she's all but an orphan?

"I-I need to get back to the kitchen."

"Elle, introduce us to your friend."

One of the blue-haired women speaks up. Elle's responding groan is quiet, but I'm close enough it's still audible to me.

She squares her shoulders, and her lips curve into a light smile. It's not complete—it doesn't reach her eyes when they meet mine—but it's still enough to cause my heartbeat to thud in my chest.

"I'll make this as quick and painless as possible."

She gestures toward the three, and we make our way to the wingback chairs they're situated in near the fireplace. Three sets of knowing eyes size me up as I approach. Three queens ready to judge their subject.

God, I hope I measure up.

"Miss Fern, Miss Fawn, Miss Merry, this is my stepbrother, Channing Kingsley. He's joining us for the holidays this year. Channing, this is Fern Myers, Fawn Carter, and Merry Andrews."

"Ladies."

I nod to each one, gently gripping each hand as it's extended, and noting the differences in each of them. While I originally thought all three to be blue-haired, only one actually is—Merry. Fawn's is a bright white, and Fern's has a pink hue only noticeable up close.

She brushes a wrinkled hand bedecked in diamond rings through the rosy locks.

"I see you eyeing my hair, young man."

"Yes, ma'am. I was just thinking to myself how stunning it is," I tell her.

She giggles.

"You're a charming one, aren't you?"

"Ma'am?"

"Enough with that nonsense. Ma'am makes me feel old. Just call me Fern and that's Fawn and Merry. None of this ma'am business with any of us. Just like we've told this one." She gestures to Elle who shakes her head.

"Miss Fern, we've been over this."

"And, honey, we've told you that the babies call us Miss. You don't have to."

"Maybe someday I'll—"

"Elle, shouldn't you check the biscuits?" Mother's voice is sharp and loud in the otherwise quiet room.

"Yes, Trudy." Elle excuses herself and disappears back down the hall.

What the fuck was that?

"That—" Merry's cheeks are bright red and partnered with pursed lips.

"Merry." Fawn nods toward me.

Merry's lips tighten further and her arms cross over her chest.

"Does that happen often?" I ask.

Mother's behavior, while normally superficial, was downright rude.

The three women stare at me for several breaths.

"It's—"

"She—"

"Elle—"

The three women begin to speak at once, stop, and sigh all in unison. It would be funny if I wasn't as concerned as I am. Regret and confusion knot my stomach.

Who have Mother and Alysa become? Maybe I should have come home sooner.

"Elle is a sweet girl. She deserves so much more than the hand she's been dealt," Fern says.

"She deserves to be swept off her feet," Merry adds.

"To have her happily ever after." Fawn lifts a finger to her lips, her blue eyes narrowing as she studies me.

"Channing, come here. I'd like you to meet someone." Mother snaps her fingers as if I'm the little dog we used to have when I was younger.

The dog didn't listen any better than I intend to.

"Ladies, it was a pleasure, but if you'll excuse me, I'd like to go see if Elle needs any help."

Fawn nods and the other two women smile, their faces brightening once more.

"Of course, dear, of course. Don't let us keep you." Fern shoos me toward the door.

"It was lovely meeting you, Channing. I'm sure we'll see you around town this season." Merry waggles her fingers.

"Lots of events, you know," Fawn says with a wink.

These three are trouble.

I have no doubt about it.

So why do I suddenly feel like a bug under their microscope?

CHAPTER 5

Elle

Tears of embarrassment burn behind my eyes, but I refuse to let them fall.

This isn't the first time Trudy has reminded me of my place. And it certainly won't be the last.

"Think about it this way, Elle, you got the escape you wanted from Charming earlier," I mumble to myself.

That sexy scent of his combined with whatever pheromones the universe had blessed him with were enough to incinerate my panties. But combined with the memories that crept in anytime he was closer than six feet from me?

I was a goner.

"Were you looking to escape from me then?" The deep voice startles me and I spin around, my heart pounding.

"Y-you followed me?"

He frowns and steps closer. Luckily the kitchen island is still between us, and my six-foot bubble I've decided I need in place around me for my sanity is maintained.

"I wanted to see if you needed any help. It doesn't look like Mother or Alysa is interested in helping you today."

"Or ever," I mumble.

"What was that?" One dark eyebrow arches and I swallow slowly.

"Nothing."

"You do it a lot. Did you know that?"

"Do what?" I ask.

His gaze is too astute for me to maintain contact with, and I turn and begin to open preserves and jams and put them in various dishes for the last of our open house menu.

He meanders—or is it swaggers—around the island to peer into the oven where the turkey for dinner tonight stays warm. Various side dishes are in the other, and his tongue darts out to lick plump lips that I personally learned are as soft as they look.

Talented too.

I don't need the reminder. But my brain and body are on a different page than my sanity at this point.

"Speak quietly. Like you don't want someone to hear you but you can't resist saying something."

It's true. A bad habit from growing up, but no one has ever called me on it.

Except him.

"I don't know what you're talking about," I deny.

He tsks and shakes his head.

"You and I both know that's not true. But if you need the reminder, when I walked in here you were talking about 'escaping Channing' and I'm curious what I did that you need an escape?"

Relief floods through me. He heard *Channing* not *Charming*. My secret is still safe.

Other than provide me with the most unforgettable night of my life?

The words push at my lips, and I cough before they can escape. Leaning my hip against the counter, I study him for several moments. He stands still, allowing my attention.

"Nothing," I say after several moments. "You're not really like Trudy and Alysa, are you?"

His lips twist in a frown that wrinkles his forehead.

"Based on what I've seen today? They've changed. I don't remember Mother and Lys being so..."

"Different?" I offer politely.

"Self-absorbed."

His eyes meet mine, and for the first time since Dad died, a sense of belonging fills me.

"They weren't always like this. I've never seen my mother act so rudely before. She treated you like you were the..." The confusion is clear in his voice.

He really doesn't know, does he?

"Help. I am."

"You're her daughter."

"*Step*daughter."

He waves away the distinction.

"You're still her family. Even if it is by marriage." He's moved closer again.

Nerves jangle under my skin, and I reach up to play with my necklace to realize yet again it's gone. Yet again, I want to kick myself for leaving it in Channing's hotel room a month ago.

Dark eyes dart to my fingers before lifting back to my face.

"Are you all right?"

I laugh off the question and drop my hand back to the counter.

"I'm fine."

"Is there anything I can do for you?"

Kiss me? Strip me naked and make me forget my own name again?

"Do you want me to take those out?" He motions to the tray where all the bowls of preserves are arranged.

Heat floods my cheeks, and I duck my head and take a

deep breath to expel the sexual tension thrumming through me.

"Oh, um, sure. Let me get the biscuits."

I give him a wide berth and walk the long way around the island to the warming oven where the biscuits have been stored. If he thinks anything is amiss, he doesn't say so, and a sigh of relief escapes my lips. If he touches me—even an innocent touch like he almost did earlier in the sitting room—I don't think I can control the words that would come out of my mouth.

And I'm pretty sure they'd all be some sort of request to repeat what he did a month ago.

Which can't happen.

I pass him the basket and avoid brushing my fingers with his. Once the basket is placed in the open spot, he lifts the tray effortlessly.

"I'll be back."

That's what I'm afraid of. The kitchen is my safe space.

"Oh—"

"I'm here. I made it. And I need a drink." Posey rushes into the kitchen and tosses her jacket in one corner before wrapping me in a hug.

Thank God she's here. She can be my excuse.

"That's okay. Posey can help me. Why don't you go visit with your mom?"

Posey's face is a mix of interest in the other occupant of the kitchen and horror at the idea of helping. The woman can't cook to save her life—she burns water. Fortunately, she keeps any comments to herself, and Channing nods.

"Sure. But let me know if I can help."

"I will," I say and paste what I hope passes for a smile on my lips.

Not.

My attention stays fixed on Channing until he turns the corner, and Posey waves her fingers in front of my face.

I blink myself out of a stupor and shift my gaze to her.

"Two questions. No, three actually. One, who the hell was that? Two, can I have him? And three, you're not serious about my help in here, right?"

The laugh that bubbles up is the first genuine laugh I've had all day.

"No, I don't expect you to help. Just keep me company. As for who he is, maybe it's time I told you about my trip to Nashville."

Her eyes light up, and she reaches for an open wine bottle beside the fridge and a glass sitting next to it. Pouring a healthy amount, she takes a large sip and boosts herself to sit on the counter.

"Tell me everything."

Posey tips her head back and hums as she takes a sip of her drink.

Her drink being more alcohol than hot chocolate? Par for the course.

The fact that she convinced me to do the same and mine is stronger than hers? Also, not surprising.

I take a small sip from my cup and almost gag as the strong peppermint liquor burns down my throat.

"So let me get this straight. Your stepbrother is a sex god."

"Shh!" I glance around, thankful we're the only two in the dark town square.

The tree is set up, ready for the lighting next week, and the garland-bedecked gazebo gleams with a semi-fresh coat of paint in the glow from the streetlight on the corner.

"What? No one's here." She spins, lifting her arms, and her hot chocolate spills.

"Is that why we're here?" I ask.

The rest of Thanksgiving had passed uneventfully, with Trudy and Alysa eating with Channing in the dining room while I excused myself with a plate in the kitchen after cleaning up from the day's festivities in the sitting room.

I wasn't able to tell Posey about Channing with all the interruptions of the holiday and she got tied up with her family with all her extended family in town for the weekend, but as of tonight, I could no longer avoid her and she stopped by the house and dragged me here.

"Would you rather we have this conversation at your house where he could hear us?"

Hot and cold flash through my body at the suggestion. No way do I want him to overhear anything. I'm too over-whelmed by the realization of my stepbrother and Charming from the masquerade ball being one and the same. And if I have my way, I'll be the only one to realize the connection. My face must show what I'm thinking since Posey nods with a smirk.

"I didn't think so."

"I think I regret telling you."

"I'm your bestie. We don't keep secrets. Remember our oath from when we were ten?"

"Yes."

We were at a sleepover—I don't remember whose house at this point—and we'd made a solemn vow to always tell each other everything.

"We were ten," I add.

"So? I tell you everything."

"A fact sometimes I wish wasn't always so detailed in its truth."

"What?" She shrugs.

"I didn't really need to know you hooked up with your professor and he likes to suck your toes," I tell her.

Red infuses her cheeks that has nothing to do with the cold.

"Don't yuck someone else's yum is what I have to say to that. We were both consenting adults."

"I'm just saying."

"And we weren't talking about me. We're talking about you shaking the sheets with your stepbrother."

"Oh my God, Posey, could you say that any louder?"

"We're alone. Nobody's here, and nobody will be here until the tree lighting next week."

I step into the gazebo and sit on the bench, shivering slightly as the chilly wood creeps through my jeans.

"I didn't realize he was my stepbrother at the time."

She sighs and sits next to me.

"I know."

"I can't avoid him forever. We're in the same house."

"I'm sure the stepmonster will ensure he stays away from you."

"But that's the thing. The more she tries to distract him, the more adamant he is to spend time with me."

"So an attractive guy wants to spend time with you."

"Yeah."

"And what's the problem?"

"He's my stepbrother. I shouldn't find him attractive."

"It's not like you grew up together." She takes a drink of her cocoa and frowns when she realizes it's empty.

I hand her mine, grateful I don't have to finish the strong mixed drink.

"No."

"So why can't you be attracted to him? He *is* attractive. Sort of like a cross between Josh Duhamel and Milo Ventimiglia."

"Kind of. But..."

"But what? Those two are my go-tos if I need a visit to my clit closet."

I choke on oxygen and my own spit.

"What?"

"What what?"

"Never mind, forget I asked."

"You were saying...but. But what?" she asks.

"He's better."

"Better as he's in your closet."

I groan.

"Posey!"

"What? At least you have actual memories of yours. Mine just exist in fantasy."

"You're no help."

She stands and tosses the two empty cups in the trash can just outside the gazebo.

"Depends on what kind of help you were looking for."

"And what help is it you're offering?" I follow her back to Main Street and we start to head back toward the bed and breakfast.

"Permission."

I pause in the middle of the sidewalk and she stops with me.

"Permission?"

"Stop thinking about what is or isn't conventionally right or wrong. Until a month ago, you'd never met him. And even then you didn't know he was who he was. If you're attracted to him, why not go after that attraction?"

"I think the shorter list is why I should."

"Life is too short." Her gaze drifts over my shoulder and lights up. "I, uh, just remembered, my mom needed me to run by the corner store for her. I need to go grab my car from the house and get there before they close. Are you okay to walk home alone?"

I eye her curiously. "We're in Mistletoe Creek. Nothing ever happens here. Of course I'm okay."

I might as well be talking to air since she's already run-walking down the sidewalk in the opposite direction.

"Bye!" I shout after her.

She lifts a hand in a wave, but doesn't turn around.

"Hello, Elle."

That sneaky bitch.

Turning around, I see why Posey's eyes lit up and why she nearly vaporized as she left. Channing stands there in a wool pea coat and black leather gloves. A half smile pops the dimple that first tipped me off as to who he is, and a layer of scruff covers his cheeks.

Definitely better.

"Hi."

"Heading home?"

I nod. "Yeah, I should probably head back."

"Maybe I can tempt you to walk with me and get a hot chocolate?"

The Mistletoe Café is just a few storefronts down.

The man could tempt a saint to sin.

And I've never been a saint.

"My treat," he says, still waiting on a response.

Life's too short. That's what Posey had said. She's right. And walking to Mistletoe Café isn't a lifelong commitment. It's a few minutes in a man's company. One who is as intriguing to me as he is attractive.

What's the harm?

"Okay."

He offers his arm to me and I loop mine through. The electricity arcs and crackles between us, and I take a deep breath. In and out.

And for the first time in a month, I allow myself to enjoy the sensation.

CHAPTER 6

Channing

H er arm slides against mine and we fall into step. Elation fizzes through my blood, driving back the cool temperatures with the small victory that isn't so small. Instead it feels like I've won the lottery.

She's been avoiding me. Since Thanksgiving, any time I walk into a room, she finds a reason to walk out. And if I'm in a room with Mother or Alysa, she doesn't walk in at all if she can help it. And the two of them cling to me like static to a balloon. After two days, I had finally convinced Mother that if she wanted me to review the bed and breakfast, I needed to focus. She'd shown me the small office behind the door across from the sitting room where I sequestered myself all afternoon with whatever files I could find.

Surprisingly, the files were organized, but all showed the same thing. A drop-off in reservations I couldn't find an explanation for. Everything I had encountered in my few days had been in good working order, and the house was spotless with the exception of Alysa's room. Yes, the house needed a face lift with its green well-worn carpet and floral wallpaper, but that didn't explain the drop-off. Did it?

The question had hounded me all afternoon, and no matter how hard I stared at the files or the office, I couldn't explain it.

The room—like the rest of the house—was dated with dark wood, burgundy leather, and a green banker's lamp so well-worn the green paint had worn away in several places. The room also held hints of fruit and floral, the scent tickling my nose and reminding me of Elle but teasing my memory of something more. It had occupied more of my concentration than I care to admit and ultimately driven me to go for a walk to clear my head.

Running into Elle had been a pleasant surprise.

"What should I order?" I ask as we approach the door.

It and the window are both decorated with garland and Christmas lights and flocked with fake snow. I wouldn't be surprised to see a little of the real stuff with as cold as it is.

It's not that cold, you baby. You're just used to tropical temperatures.

"What do you normally like?" She looks up, her eyes catching the streetlamp, and the tip of her nose and cheeks are a light pink in the chilly air.

The corner of my lips lift in a smile.

"Usually as much caffeine as I can. But I doubt that's a good idea tonight."

She shakes her head.

"Not if you want to sleep."

I'm still recovering from jet lag so I'll pass on caffeine. Reaching out, I pull the door open and allow her to precede me into the building. The loss of the physical connection is immediate, and my hand itches to drop to the small of her back and reestablish the connection as she approaches the counter.

There aren't many people inside—a few customers and a barista behind the counter. But just like when I walked into the sitting room, everything around me stops. The handful of people openly stare, and I have to stop myself from checking my fly.

Elle motions me forward, and the rest of the world unfreezes even though the heat from the stares still singes the back of my neck as I approach the counter.

"Hi, Elle. What can I fix for you?"

The cashier can't be any older than sixteen, and her pen hovers over the pad, ready to write

the order.

"Hi, Missy. How about a Chai Latte?"

"Sure thing. What about you?"

Two gazes shift to me and I shrug.

"Elle, how about you pick for me?"

She studies me for a second, and I wish I could hear her thoughts as the gears visibly turn.

"Hmm, he'll have a salted caramel hot chocolate."

The teen scratches my order onto her pad below Elle's and walks to the fancy coffee machine out of place in a town like Mistletoe Creek.

With a few presses of a button, the entire machine whirs to life.

Missy turns to me and smiles. "Mom said to tell you thanks for the muffins the next time I see you."

"Muffins?" I ask.

"Missy's mom has been going through a hard time. I made them a batch of muffins for the holiday weekend." Elle's voice is quiet, almost inaudible over the loud noise. But she raises her voice to be heard by the young barista. "You're welcome."

"How do you know all this? Are you friends with her mom or something?"

She lifts a shoulder and lets it drop, setting her blonde hair swinging along the lapels of her jacket. I have the urge to finger the strand, to see if it's as silky as it looks while I tuck it behind her ear.

"Not really, but I know her. It's a small town."

No shit.

The evidence of how small still builds heat in my shoulder blades. I turn quickly, but neither of the customers behind me are caught staring.

"They were just looking," Elle tells me with a conspiratorial wink.

"So it's not just me?"

The small smile she gives me makes me want to have her smile all the time.

"It is, but not the way you think. You're news. People are curious about you."

"I'd rather they weren't."

"You get used to it. Most of the time people mean well."

Missy interrupts our conversation to hand us our drinks.

"That'll be $8.50."

I pull out my wallet despite Elle's protests.

"I asked you to walk with me, remember?" I ask and hand the teenager a twenty. "Keep the change. Do you mind if we walk?"

I motion toward the door and Elle nods.

"Sure." The relief in her voice is tangible and we make our way back outside.

I take a sip of the hot chocolate and hum as the sweet and salty flavors dance along my tongue.

She stares at me, her mouth partially open and the cup almost touching her lips.

"What?"

"N-nothing." She walks away, heading in the opposite direction of the bed and breakfast.

What was that?

It only takes me a few strides to catch up to her, my height working at an advantage despite her quick steps.

"You sure?" I ask.

"Uh-huh." She takes a drink.

"I feel like I don't know anything about you."

"There's not much to say." Her attention stays focused ahead as we make our way down the quiet Main Street.

"I doubt that. Are you from here?"

She glances at me for a moment before taking another drink.

"Born and raised."

It fits her, but I keep the comment to myself.

"And the bed and breakfast?"

"Mom and Dad opened it when my mom was pregnant with me. They were both from Knoxville and wanted to settle down in a small town."

"How'd they pick here?" I ask as we turn down a side street dotted with houses, some already donned with Christmas lights.

She laughs.

"They liked the town name. Mistletoe. It reminded Mom how she and my dad met at a Christmas party."

"Is it always so...festive?" I ask and gesture to the lights.

"No. But we have our fair share of holidays and festivities. But Christmas is when it shines. All the holiday events and decorations. It's magical. I've never seen it anywhere else."

"You sound like you speak from experience."

"I lived in Knoxville when I started college. Took some time off when my mom got sick. My dad convinced me I needed to go back. Finish my degree."

"What did you study?"

"Tourism and hospitality management."

"So the B&B runs pretty deep, huh?"

"Yeah. It was always the plan for Mom and Dad to turn it over to me at some point. Then Mom got sick, and Dad told me there was plenty of time. Now your Mom owns it. She owns my dream."

"Is she the one who named it The Glass Slipper?"

"No, that was my mom. She loved all the old fairy tales. Always told me I was her happily ever after. Me and my dad. Cinderella was her favorite."

"Elle," I say and watch her nod again.

"I don't think my dad would have agreed to Cinderella."

"Her real name was Ella anyway," I tell her as the fairy tale comes back to me. "Cinder was only because she slept near a fireplace to stay warm."

She stops to stare at me.

"Lys loved that story when she was little, so I used to read it to her."

"You're full of surprises," she tells me.

"I could say the same thing about you."

"How so?"

We start to walk again and make another turn with more houses and more Christmas lights.

"When Mother asked me here for the holidays, I don't know what I expected."

"I can only imagine what she said about me," she mumbles.

"Not much," I hedge.

Mother had plenty to say about her. Very little was complimentary.

"Liar."

"Have you ever thought about going somewhere else?"

She's quiet for several breaths, the only sound the dull thud of our shoes against the sidewalk.

"This is home," she says after several moments of silence. "My friends are here. Mostly. I mean, Posey lives in Charlotte, but she still comes back a few times a year. The B&B is my home. If I left...it would feel like I was losing my parents all over again."

Her eyes are glassy when she glances over at me again. I stop and put a hand on her arm to keep her still.

"I didn't mean to make you upset."

She sniffles and swipes at the moisture under her eyes. I want to tell her that she may not have a choice. Mother is thinking of selling the bed and breakfast since it's not turning a profit anymore. But I don't want to add to the sadness visible even in the dim light of the porch lights around us.

The smile she gives me trembles around the edges.

"I know."

Fuck.

I yank her to me and she crashes against my chest. My arms wrap around her naturally, and as much comfort as I wanted to give with this embrace, the sense of rightness with her in my arms is something I can't ignore.

How is it possible when I've only just met her?

And what about Cinderella?

Cinderella was a Halloween hookup. A night I won't forget, but not one I want to put my life on hold for anymore. Elle is flesh and blood and *real* in my arms.

"I'm sorry," I murmur and lift my hands to rub up and down her back.

Her slight grip on the wool at my back tightens, and her deep breath exhales into the night in a puff of air before she releases her fingers. I'm not ready to break the contact with her and tighten my arms.

"You have nothing to be sorry for. You've..." She lifts her head, her voice trailing off as her dark eyes meet mine.

Moisture still sparkles on her lashes, but it's her lips that capture my attention. They part under my focus, and her tongue slips out to slick along the outside. My body hardens in a painful rush. Given how close she is to me, I have little doubt she realizes the impact her nearness has on me, especially when her eyes widen slightly.

"I've...?" I prompt, but couldn't tell anyone what we were talking about if asked.

Instead I could clearly describe the multiple shades of pink and blush that combine to make her lips enticing, tempting me to close the distance. I close my eyes and swallow hard, but the image isn't eliminated. Light notes of jasmine and gardenia become stronger and wrap around us and transport us from the dark street to a tropical paradise.

She shakes her head, a wrinkle forming between her brows.

"I forget. We should head back."

She pulls away farther, and my arms operate involuntarily, holding her in place.

"Wait."

"For what?"

"You have to feel this too, Elle. I can't be alone in how attracted to you I am."

"You're my stepbrother." She says it like it's enough of an explanation.

Maybe. Maybe not.

"So what?"

"It's wrong."

"What's so wrong about it? We're two consenting adults. It's not like we met as kids. I just met you."

"I know. But none of that makes it not wrong."

"You're not saying you aren't attracted to me," I point out.

"I'm not."

I can't help but smile at her obvious lie. Her lower body is still pressed against mine even if her upper body is farther away. And she's not pulling away, but staying where she is.

"You and I both know that's not true." I squeeze her against me to prove my point.

Her moan is a breath of sound, but enough for me to press further.

"What are you afraid of?"

"Nothing." She bristles.

"If you're not attracted to me, prove it."

"Prove it how?"

"Kiss me."

"How will that prove anything?"

"If you kiss me and you aren't attracted to me, I'll know this is one-sided. I'll leave you alone."

She rolls her eyes and rises on her tiptoes. "Fine."

"Don't you want to know what happens when our kiss proves my point?"

"It won't."

I keep talking and ignore her muttered denial.

"When our kiss proves my point, I want you to admit you aren't telling the truth."

"So what are you waiting for?" she challenges, and fuck, do I love this side of her.

The sassy side. The sweet side. The side that pushes me away and the one that pulls me closer.

I lift my hand and drag my finger along her jaw while wishing my gloves were gone and it was skin to skin. From her chin and back until I can cup her nape and knead the tight flesh. Her eyes flutter shut, and her moan is louder this time. Her lips part and I don't waste the opportunity. Dropping my lips to hers, I explore slowly. Small kisses from one corner to another, teasing nips until I settle my mouth more fully on hers.

I capture her gasp of breath, taking advantage of her parted lips to dip my tongue to tangle with hers. She trails her hands up the front of my jacket, her arms twining around my neck and her hands gripping more fully as she pushes flush against my chest. Her tongue teases mine, and I use my hand at her nape to shift her into a different position, to deepen the kiss. I drop my other hand from her waist to her hip, tracing it back until I can palm her ass and tug her farther against my erection.

But she doesn't pull away. Just the opposite. She lifts her leg to wrap around my hip, to pull herself even closer. Stars dot my vision and my lungs burn for oxygen, but I don't break the kiss, relishing each new experience kissing her brings.

The little sounds, the way her body fits perfectly against mine. Her taste mixed with the scents of floral and fruit.

I rip my mouth from hers, my eyes springing open.

"Cinderella?" I ask, breathing hard as my body attempts to replenish the oxygen I've deprived it of.

Her own eyes are open wide, pupils dilated with a mix of desire and...surprise?

"Elle," she says, her gaze shifting to something over my right shoulder.

Struggling through a lust-filled fog, I'm slowly clicking the puzzle pieces into place. I drop my arms and step back, and the cool air clears the rest of the fog.

"No. You're Cinderella. Halloween."

"I-I don't know what you're talking about."

"Nashville. The hospitality conference. There was a masquerade ball."

Why am I telling her stuff she already knows? It *has* to be her.

"That wasn't me."

Her fingers lift to her neck again, searching for something. Looking for the necklace she must fidget with. The one in my shaving kit even now.

"But—"

"We kissed, Channing. And it was great. I'm not going to

lie. I am attracted to you. But this?" She motions between the two of us. "Can't happen."

"The hell it can't." I reach for her and she steps back.

"I need to get back. I have to be up early tomorrow. Goodnight."

She turns and is halfway down the block before I speak.

"I don't even know where I am," I call after her.

"The B&B is one more left turn that way." She thumbs in the direction she was walking.

"What if I take a wrong turn?" I ask.

"It's a small town; no one gets lost."

With that, she all but sprints down the sidewalk toward the direction she pointed.

I take my time, allowing her the space she so desperately wants while I go over everything I know.

My lips still tingle with the kiss, and I lift my hand to rub against them.

Blonde hair. Dark eyes.

The shocked expression on her face the morning of my arrival.

Gardenia and jasmine.

My pillow smelled like that the next morning when I woke up to find her gone.

The sensation that I had known her forever.

The magnetic pull she has on me.

Her continued search for something around her neck that wasn't there. But should be.

Climbing the steps to the front porch, I let myself in. I'm on the second tread when Mother's voice calls to me from the sitting room.

"Where were you?"

It's been many years since I owed her an explanation. And I for damn sure am not starting now.

"Out."

"With Elle?"

I have no reason to lie.

"Yes."

"She's not right for you."

"That's funny, I thought that was my decision," I tell her.

"She's your stepsister. What would people say?"

"Mother, I stopped caring about what people think of me a long time ago."

"The town is already talking," she counters.

"I highly doubt that."

"She's leaving."

A record scratches through my churning thoughts.

"What?"

Mother nods.

"She is. She's been looking for a job in Nashville. She wants to leave all this behind." She waves her hand around the sitting room.

The tears were genuine earlier. There's not a doubt in my mind.

"What makes you think so?"

"She came back from that hospitality conference this year different."

Click.

"Different how?" I ask.

"Unfocused, not working as hard, easily distracted. Probably moving back in with her fiancé."

"Fiancé?"

Elle hadn't mentioned one before I challenged her to kiss me. Surely, she would have.

"Mother, have you told Elle the B&B isn't turning a profit anymore? That you wanted me to come check it out to decide if you should sell it?"

"Why would I need to do that?" Her confusion is genuine.

"This is her home," I tell her.

"Mark left it to me."

Why would he have only left it to Mother? Elle would have been of age. A headache is blooming in the back of my neck, and I lift a hand to rub at the spot.

"I'm going to bed," Mother says and stands from her chair.

I trail behind her quietly, still cataloging everything from the night.

The pleasant surprise of seeing her outside the B&B.

The genuine conversation as we walked along the quiet streets.

The kiss I could no longer resist.

"Goodnight, Channing," Mother says and opens her bedroom door.

"Goodnight. Oh, Mother?"

"Yes?"

"Does Elle wear a necklace?"

"She used to. A drab little chain her father gave her. He said something about the chip of a diamond belonging to his first wife. I refused to let him get away with that when he proposed to me."

I don't bother to remind her about how small her engagement ring was from Dad.

"What do you mean used to?" I ask, even though I already know.

"She hasn't since she got back from Nashville. She probably sold it."

"Goodnight," I say again and wait for her to step into her room and close the door.

Walking to my own room, I go straight into the en suite bathroom and grab my shaving kit off the counter. I lift the old chain out of the bag gently, staring at the ring centered on

71

the thin strand. One with a small diamond and one plain wedding band with an inscription inside.

Happily ever after.

Maybe it was time I reunited the necklace with its owner.

"I'm coming for you, sweets."

CHAPTER 7

Elle

The one good thing about running a bed and breakfast? Eventually, my body was used to getting up early.

The bad thing about running a bed and breakfast? I'm staring at my ceiling at 4:30 in the morning when I could be sleeping. And I should still be sleeping after tossing and turning all night—my dreams invaded by memories of my night with Channing and our kiss last night.

The way his fingers had cupped my chin, his thumb rubbing along my jawline while his tongue mastered mine. Memory had *not* exaggerated how good of a kisser he was. I'd been ready to melt into a puddle at his feet last night. Until he realized who I was.

Isn't that a good thing?

"No. No, it's not," I say out loud in an attempt to drown out those kinds of thoughts.

Now that he knew who I was, I suspect he won't be as easy to avoid.

So don't avoid. Kiss.

I groan and throw back the covers to cool my overheated

skin. Maybe the cold will clear the temporary insanity of wanting to kiss him again. I can't repeat last night, no matter how badly my body craves his.

The fact that he is my stepbrother is enough. Or at least it should be even if my body doesn't seem to care about the label. If that isn't enough, the man lives out of a suitcase and has for years.

Mistletoe Creek is my home. This building is my last connection to my parents. The plan had always been for me to finish school and come home to take over running the inn. It meant retirement for my parents and making the updates and changes I wanted to entice more visitors. But the universe had a funny way of screwing up that plan. Not just once, but twice.

Have you ever thought about going somewhere else?

Channing's question echoes louder than any other thought.

The truth was, I had. After Dad had died. The day Trudy told me she owned the inn. Or when she told me she wanted to add to the guest rooms. But instead of converting the rooms we had earmarked, she wanted me to move out of my room. Days when the demands from Trudy and Alysa competed with the long list of other things I had to do to keep the B&B running.

But on those days, I'd run into someone I had known my whole life, someone who had known my parents. They'd share a memory of them when they first started the inn or at some point of its little history, and it would remind me why I wanted to stay and give me the strength to keep going.

"If we don't book some guests soon, though, nothing will be left to stay for," I mumble.

I can't understand it.

Consistent reservations had suddenly stopped. The few bookings for November and December from our regulars had canceled with no reason given. Is it us? Or is it impacting other businesses in tourism as well?

The annual report I picked up at the conference a month ago might shed some light on the situation. It—along with all the other information I gathered—had been tossed in the office when I got back to a house Alysa and Trudy had trashed in my absence.

"Well, if I'm up, I might as well be productive."

Swinging my legs to the side, I sit up and reach for my hoodie before slipping my feet into fuzzy boots to combat the chill along the floorboards.

The house is quiet when I make my way down the stairs from my room, but I still creep past Channing's door in stealth mode. I can hardly handle the man with caffeine. I don't need to attempt it without coffee. Especially when memories of our night together swim just below the surface.

In the kitchen, the coffeemaker reflects the light I left on above the stove. I don't bother with any other lights since my plan involves getting my drink and going over the paperwork in the office. I could probably find my way in this room in the pitch dark. At times I have. The machine does its thing while I stare out the window into the dark, chilly morning where frost sparkles on the grass. When I was a little girl, Mom told me it was fairies covering the world in diamond dust.

"Because they loved the sparkle," I murmur and turn to doctor the dark liquid in my mug.

She told me that fairy tales existed and Dad and I were proof they did because she got her happily ever after.

"Only it wasn't ever after," I say.

Mug in hand, I make my way across the hall to Dad's office.

"Oh."

My fingers tighten around the handle on the mug a split second before I drop it.

"Good morning," Channing says from behind the desk.

The husky quality of his voice creates a ripple of awareness down my spine. He looks like he belongs behind the solid wooden desk—hair mussed from sleep, a pair of glasses resting on his nose and highlighting the dark brown of his eyes.

"You wear glasses?"

Because that's a normal response to *good morning*. I can't help it. The man in all his sleepy sexiness scrambles my brain.

His damn dimple makes an appearance next to lips I need to stop thinking about kissing.

"Sometimes. When my eyes are tired. Usually only happens with computer screens, but this is something else." He lifts a thick, green-covered notebook.

A smile tugs at my lips.

"That was my dad's."

"He kept good records, even if the handwriting is better meant for Thumbelina's eyesight than mine."

I move a step closer. A part of me wants to snatch the book away. To protect the pieces of Dad that still exist. His tiny writing was a holdover from the way he learned in elementary school, and I can almost picture him bent over the notebook, eyes and fingers focused on the minuscule writing.

"Why are you looking at his records?"

"Mother asked me to."

"Why?"

"She thought maybe I could help. You already know I do this kind of thing for a living."

"Is that why you were in Nashville?" The question is out before I can stop it.

Neither of us needs to be reminded of what happened in Nashville.

He stands and stretches his arms above his head with a groan. The gray T-shirt rides up and reveals a strip of skin between it and his plaid pajama pants. Skin I've felt next to mine. Is it hot in here?

"A friend of mine was supposed to speak. She had a conflict and called me to cover since I had planned on attending anyway."

Jealousy pinches my stomach. I have no claim on him—I don't want one—so why do I care who his friend is?

Channing moves from behind the desk and closes more of the distance between us.

"She and her partner got word that their adoption application had been accepted," he explains. "There's no need to be jealous."

I suck in a breath at how easily he can read me. I don't like it. But if he realizes, he doesn't let on. Instead he plucks the coffee cup from my grip and takes a long drink.

"Hey, that's mine." I lunge for the cup and press against him when he holds it out of reach.

My body lights up at the innocent contact, my nipples pebbling against the thick cotton of my sweatshirt.

"Sharing is caring," he tells me, banding one arm around my waist and holding me in place.

Based on the twinkle in his eyes, he planned this.

"Channing." I try to make his name sound like a warning, but it comes out too breathy.

"I like my real name on your lips, even though Charming was close," he murmurs and fixates his attention to my mouth.

Heat travels through my body, igniting every nerve to beg for his touch.

"Why are you doing this?"

"Because I haven't been able to get you off my mind. Not since I woke up and found myself alone. Fuck, not since the moment I saw you in the ballroom."

"It was only one night."

"Are you telling me that's all you want? You've been able

to forget me so easily?" The fire in his eyes as they search mine burns through the lie resting on my tongue.

"I..."

"You haven't stopped thinking about it either. Have you, Elle?"

I sink my teeth into my lip to stem the words, but my body betrays me with a shake of my head.

"Do you think about me when you touch yourself? Pretend it's my hands on your body the same way I remember your hands on mine?"

I whimper at the images he conjures.

"Tell me," he demands.

"Yes." I meet his gaze and trail my hands up to link my hands behind his neck.

The move presses my breasts more against his chest, and the friction drives my need for him higher.

"Kiss me," I tell him.

I don't wait for his response and pull him down even as he lowers his head. Our mouths meet in a fiery explosion of fire-works and sensation with a direct line to my core. Channing's tongue traces along my lips, and I open to allow him to take complete control of our kiss as my pussy throbs under the onslaught.

His arm tightens around my waist and arches me farther against him. I'm only vaguely aware of the thud of the mug hitting the thick desk before his other hand grips my ass and squeezes.

I break the kiss on a mewl, my head tipping back on my shoulders. He takes advantage and drops his lips to my neck, finding the sensitive spot just below my earlobe. Shifting my hands to his hair, I hold him in place. He nips at my earlobe, and my knees buckle with pleasure.

Without missing a beat, he boosts me into his arms until

my legs wrap around his waist. He pulses his hips, rubbing his erection against the center seam of my pants.

He groans and his fingers flex against my thighs.

"Let me," he growls.

His lips continue their assault on my jaw, neck, and ear.

The rational part of me knows what I should say.

That side of you wouldn't be kissing your stepbrother.

Touché.

"Elle." My name is a vibration against my skin and travels through my body to obliterate rational thought.

I don't even know what he wants me to agree to.

Do you care?

Memories of our night together flash through my body and leave nothing but heat in their wake.

"Yes."

CHAPTER 8

Channing

The word is almost too quiet, but it's one I've waited for her to say. Not just since last night and not only because she's Cinderella. Even before I knew who she was, a magnetism existed I couldn't ignore. The need to claim her, to make her mine—I've never felt those outside the night with her a month ago.

I find the tendon at the base of her neck and shoulder and sink my teeth roughly into the spot, relishing the way my name breaks on her lips. Her hips shift against mine where she rubs her center over my erection.

Upstairs. Get her upstairs.

I'm not sure if it's my mind or my dick leading the interaction here, but regardless, upstairs is too far away and presents too many challenges—namely Mother and Alysa. Neither of them needs to be a part of this moment or stop it from happening.

A few steps to the door and I'm able to push it closed, fumbling blindly with the lock until it engages before I retrace my steps all the way behind the desk. I lower her slowly and knead my fingers into the ample flesh of her hips while I struggle under the power of the desire she inspires. She blinks her eyes open, and the dark depths remind me of melted chocolate. The fire in them reflects the inferno burning in me, and I steady my hands to keep from ripping her clothes off the way my body demands.

"You're sure?"

The need to claim, to kiss, to lose myself in her again wraps my fingers around the hem of her hoodie as lust snarls against the thin thread of control I keep over it.

She nods, and I'm mesmerized by the way her tongue slicks out to rim her lips in a sheen of moisture.

"Yes."

I can taste the word still on the luscious pink of her mouth when I dip my head again, pleasantries be damned as I push my tongue to dance with hers. The tips of her fingers dig into the back of my biceps, and the small pricks of pain confirm this isn't a dream. Her legs tighten around my waist and force my erection against the heat of her pussy, evident despite the thin layers of cotton separating us.

I tilt her head with mine, deepening the kiss as I start to tug her sweatshirt up, dragging my fingers along smooth warm skin along her stomach and the sides of her breasts. Her chest bumps forward, seeking my fingers with more than just a quick touch, but I keep my hands moving until I have to break the kiss to pull both the sweatshirt and her T-shirt up and off.

"Fuck," I groan at the sight she makes in front of me, battling to keep my eyes open to take in her ample breasts and the rose peaks that tip them both.

They tighten under my gaze, begging for my lips, and I dip my head to oblige.

Circling one bud with my tongue, I drag her nipple into my mouth while I lift my fingers to tug at the other one.

She cries out and falls back to her elbows on the desk. Her new position grants me better access, and I move with her, lowering my body into the cradle of her thighs while I lavish first one and then the other breast with the attention of my lips, tongue, and teeth.

"I should have spent more time on these," I mumble against the soft skin before I nip at the peak close to my lips.

Her body spasms with the caress, and I repeat it again on the opposite breast and enjoy the way both her fingers tighten in my hair at the same time her legs constrict around my waist.

The first time in the hotel on Halloween had been more focused on the frenzied pleasure of the two of us exploding together. The other times during our night together had been slower, but still no less focused on the end goal—hearing her come. But this time? This time I am going to take my time. To make her break apart incrementally until I sink into her and we both shatter.

"What do you think, sweets?" My nickname for her slips out, but it's true.

She's sweeter than my favorite dessert and I can't get enough.

"I think you're trying to drive me crazy," she says through panting breaths.

Her hips shift between my hips and the desk, and my dick presses against the seam of my pajama pants. I'm surprised it doesn't rip through the thin fabric. I groan and lower my hips farther, holding her in place.

"The only place I'm trying to drive you is to ecstasy," I tell her and pull her nipple back into my mouth, hollowing my cheeks as I suck.

Her hips bump against mine with nowhere to go and she cries out.

"You're—oh god—you're going too slow. I don't—"

I release her nipple with a pop and admire my handiwork of the tight, red bud still damp from my mouth.

"You do. I'm going to take as long as I like. I won't be rushed again."

"A-again?"

"One night was not nearly enough with you."

"But—"

"Do you like what I'm doing right now?" I ask.

"Yes." The admission is breathy and her breasts quiver with her nod.

"Do you want me to stop?"

"No."

"Should I keep going?" I lick along her nipple and she moans.

"*Yes.*"

I turn back to her breasts, peppering kisses from one tip to the other while I work to unravel her legs from my waist and start to tug her pajama pants off her hips.

"Up."

Her body instantly follows my command, and I move back, dragging her pants with me until she's spread naked on top of the desk. She lifts her feet and props them on the edge of the desk, dropping her knees open. Her face is all mischief when I tear my gaze away to meet hers.

"Still up to your same old tricks, huh?"

"I don't know what you mean."

"You're trying to push my buttons."

"Is it working?" The end of her question comes out in a squeak as I trail one of my hands from her instep to her inner thigh.

She holds her breath, but I keep my hand where it is for several moments before dragging it back down.

"What do you think?"

I palm my erection and squeeze, trying to ease the ache in my balls and hold on to the control she plays with.

"Obviously, I'm not doing a good job if we're having a conversation."

Her hand begins to inch between her legs, and I lift one brow.

"What happened the last time?"

"You don't have a belt this time."

"Fuck, you have a sassy mouth when you let it show."

"Maybe you should do something about it," she challenges.

Between one breath and the next, I'm holding her wrists on either side of her hips as I lean over her, my mouth fusing to hers.

Her tongue chases mine when I retreat, breaking the kiss to drag my lips along her jaw. She moans as I press hot, open-mouthed kisses against her neck and collarbone, and I continue to move south. Two kisses to each breast before I drop my lips to the underside of her breasts, her stomach, and dip my tongue into her navel.

"I want—"

"I know what you want."

Releasing her hands, I thread my fingers with hers and squeeze, dropping smaller kisses as I move unerringly lower. Her fingers squeeze mine and she lifts her hips again, pressing up on her feet wrapped around the edge of the desk.

"Please," she begs.

My only response is to nuzzle the space between where her hip and thigh join. The scent of her arousal is another snap to the thread of my control, and the deep breath I take only makes my dick press harder against my pants.

Maybe I should take them off. But it would mean stepping away, and I don't think I'm physically capable of doing that right now. I lick the line of her pussy from back to front, and her hips jump against my mouth. She tastes even better than I remember, and I lift our joined hands to her breasts before releasing her fingers.

"Play with those beautiful breasts for me."

Her fingers immediately comply, and I drop my hands to hold her thighs open and strengthen my focus on her pussy. Flattening my tongue, I repeat the back to forward caress and find her clit to tap it with my tongue.

"*Channing.*"

Fuck, the way my name sounds on her lips as her pleasure continues to build is enough to have me almost coming in my pants like a preteen boy. I grunt and circle the hard nub with my tongue. I shift my hands and bring one up to press a finger into her wet heat. Her muscles clamp around the digit—she's so fucking close.

"Please, please, please." She repeats the word over and over, her hips shifting as she tries to grind herself against my finger and tongue.

I curve my finger until I find the spot that has her body spasming and her walls clenching my finger even harder. Bingo. Rubbing along the spot, I wrap my lips around her clit and suck while tapping my tongue repeatedly against it.

Her hips levitate off the desk, pressing against me as her orgasm swamps her. She cries out, the loudest sound she's made so far this morning, and I move my finger in and out as I work her through her orgasm and continue to rotate my tongue where it is. Her walls continue to grip my finger until her body relaxes, and her hips drop as the orgasm ebbs.

"It's too much," she says and tries to shy away from my mouth, and I shift back and stand from my crouch.

Her hands are on her stomach, and the redness of the tips of her breasts tell me just how hard she was playing with them as I worked her through one orgasm. The rest of her is a rosy hue, and her eyes are soft and dreamy.

"Do you know how fucking beautiful you are?" I ask her.

She shakes her head.

"No."

"If you only knew how many times I thought of doing this again."

"How many?" she asks.

"More than I care to admit," I grumble and lean over to grab her lips in another kiss. Her fingers tangle in my hair and hold me to her, and she tastes herself on my tongue as her legs wrap back around my waist.

"More," she says and breaks the kiss.

"More?"

My brain is struggling to stay engaged in the conversation with all the blood rushing to my dick.

"I want you inside me."

My dick is on board one hundred percent, but I can't help but tease her.

"Oh, you do, do you?"

She nods.

"Who do you want?"

"You."

"Tell me."

"Please. I want you to fuck me."

I yank at the waistband of my pants until my cock springs free. The instant relief of not being held by cotton is a heady rush that comes with a reminder.

"Fuck. Condom." I've never thought about carrying around a condom in my pajama pants before, but I better fucking start.

I shift and her legs lock around my waist and pull me dangerously close.

"I'm on birth control," she tells me.

"You're sure?" I ask, gritting my teeth as my dick slides through her folds.

"I—yes."

I notch my head at her opening and keep my eyes on hers as I begin to press forward. Her eyes widen and she freezes.

"What's wrong?" I ask.

Her eyes dart back toward the door before she turns them back to me.

"Is the door locked?"

"Yes, but—"

"Shhh." Her hands come up to cover my mouth and we're both still.

Only then do I make out the creak of the floorboard in the hallway.

"Elle, where are you?" Mother's voice is sharp and closer than I would like.

The handle rattles on the office door, and a panic-stricken expression crosses Elle's face.

"I-I'm in here," she calls out. "I'll be out in just a minute."

"Why is the door locked?"

I arch a brow and wait for her to figure out a response.

"I-uh-I'm not sure. It must just be the handle. It's happened before, and as soon as I open it from in here it'll be fine."

"Hurry up."

My muscles tighten at Mother's impatient tone.

"I'll be right there. I can bring your coffee up if you'd like?"

"I don't want that drivel you drink. I want coffee from the café."

"O-okay. I'll run and grab some. I'll be back soon."

"See that you are. I'm going back to bed until you come back."

Another creak of the floorboards is followed by the dull thuds of Mother's steps on the stairs. There's the distant squeak of a door hinge followed by the door closing. Only once it's closed does Elle drop her hands from my mouth.

"Where were we?" I ask.

She shakes her head.

"I'm sorry. I can't."

What the hell?

She drops her legs from my waist and shifts off the desk, grimacing as several papers stick to her ass.

"What the hell just happened?"

She gathers her clothes and slips them back on without looking at me.

"Elle?"

"I'll make it up to you," she promises and lifts on her tiptoes to press a kiss to my cheek.

"Make what up to me?" I ask.

"I know you're mad we had to stop..." She turns to walk toward the door and I reach out a hand and wrap it around her bicep.

"I'm not mad." Even if my dick is.

"Oh."

"You know you don't have to be at her beck and call whenever she demands something."

"She's my boss. She could say at any moment she's not happy and I need to leave."

"Has she said something like that before?"

She won't meet my eyes and I have my answer.

Son of a bitch.

"I'm sorry. I have to go."

She tugs her arm from my grasp and is at the door before I can stop her again.

"We're not done talking about this."

She doesn't answer, and I'm left alone in the office. I could almost swear I dreamed the whole encounter. But her taste still lingers on my tongue.

"It's time I get to the bottom of this shit show."

But which shit show? I thought I was coming to fix the bed and breakfast. But

there's a bigger problem to fix.

Now where the hell do I start?

CHAPTER 9

Channing

> Do you know what it's liked to be
> cockblocked by your own mother?

With every fucking little thing she could think of to keep me from tracking down Elle and finishing what we started the other morning. It's like she fucking knows. For the last several days, anytime I've mentioned Elle to my mother, she bristled like a cat near a bathtub and came up with something I had to help her with right away to keep me from seeking out the one woman I wanted to see.

HAYDEN

LMAO.

Not since I was 17.

I hate you.

After the morning with Elle in the office, I told Hayden.

I found Cinderella.

And she was my stepsister.

He thought it was hysterical. I begged to differ.

> Maybe coming home for the holidays was a bad idea.

When I booked my flight, I had this vision of coming back to Tennessee to experience some kitschy, family holiday movie while helping Mother figure out what was wrong with the B&B.

It was not—as she continued to try to convince me—Elle's fault. Mother described Elle as lazy, unintelligent, and self-centered.

Everything I had witnessed the last few days screamed the opposite. It was Elle's hard work that kept this place running even while she catered to Mother and Alysa.

She owns my dream.

What Elle said continued to nag at me. Why would her father not include her in the ownership of her family legacy?

> You could always come here.

> Why? I thought you said it was moving along.

> The developers are wooing the owner.

> They treated him and his wife to an all-expenses paid weekend at their resort.

> Fuck. They must really want that property.

> How do I compete with that?

> You don't. We don't compete with the bigwigs. We explain why he opened the business to begin with.

> I don't think he likes me.

> For Christ's sake, it's not about that.

> You may need to come here.

The idea had my body revolting. I wasn't ready to walk away from Elle. For more reasons than just finishing what we started the other day.

> I will if I have to.

> But I need more time here.

> I'll see what I can do.

Pocketing my phone, I leave my room and head downstairs to find Mother and Alysa in the sitting room.

"Where's Elle?" I ask.

Alysa snorts and barely shifts her attention from the phone in her hand. "Who cares?"

Mother's eyes narrow, her lips pursing as she studies me. Despite the bug under a microscope feeling, I refuse to fidget, and hold her gaze until she finally looks away.

"Breakfast is in the kitchen if that's what you're looking for."

Because that's the only reason I should be looking for Elle. She doesn't say it out loud, but the message is clear in her voice.

My teeth click together and I attempt to relax my jaw. I'm not looking for breakfast. I ate hours ago since it's now past noon.

"I'm not hungry. I had a question about the B&B."

Liar, liar, pants on fire.

I don't have a question for her about the inn. Or, at least, it's not my primary reason for seeking her out.

"I can answer your questions," Mother says.

I doubt it. But I keep my comment to myself.

"Who is the attorney who worked through the ownership piece of Mark's will?"

"Why?"

"I have a question and want to review the agreement."

"I own the inn. Mark left it to me." The defensiveness in her voice grates on my nerves.

If this were a job, I would have walked away by now.

"I'm not questioning the ownership, Mother. I'm trying to ensure that all the paperwork is in order."

But a small part of me questions the legitimate ownership and claims she's making.

"Gepetto Snow worked with Mark on all that."

"Thank you, I'll give him a call."

"He died."

Oh, for fuck's sake. I refrain from rolling my eyes—barely. These continued roadblocks she keeps tossing up are wearing thin.

"Who took over?"

"Took over what?"

"The legal dealings," I practically growl.

She's completely nonplussed while my temper is hanging by a frayed thread.

"I have the name upstairs. I'll look it up once we get back." She shrugs one of her shoulders.

"Back from where?" I lift a hand to the back of my neck and rub at the tension headache building there.

"Alysa and I need you to take us shopping in Knoxville."

"What's wrong with the shops here?"

There aren't many, but I did notice a half dozen storefronts on my walk with Elle the other night.

Mother and Alysa stare at me as if what I suggested is the equivalent of hell on earth.

"We don't shop *here*," Alysa says, wrinkling her nose.

"We prefer Nashville—"

"I'm not driving you to Nashville to go shopping," I tell Mother.

"Which is why Knoxville will have to do. Lysa, grab our coats."

With a long-suffering sigh, my sister grabs her coat and hands Mother hers.

"What about Elle?" I ask.

"What about her?"

"Does she want to come?"

I wouldn't blame her if she didn't, but isn't it polite to at least ask?

"Why would she want to come?" Lysa sneers.

I want to shake some manners into her. When did she become this person?

"Because—"

"She has work to do," Mother interrupts.

I want to tell her they can go themselves. I'll stay back and help Elle.

But the promise I made to Dad before he passed and my own manners win out over what I want to do.

Grabbing my coat, I usher them to the door, praying for patience to handle an afternoon with the two of them and

95

vowing to talk to Elle by the end of the day. No matter what.

Hours later and several hundred dollars lighter, I pull into the drive of the bed and breakfast to the welcoming glow of the porch light.

Finally.

I'm exhausted. Mother and Alysa dragged me to one store after another before convincing me I needed to treat them to dinner after purchasing mountains of clothes, shoes, and makeup for the both of them for Christmas.

"I'm going to leave this here. I'm wiped out. Elle can bring it in for me." Alysa opens the back door and leaves the stack of bags behind.

"You will not," I tell her, my patience at the breaking point. "You wanted all that crap, you can take it inside."

"But she always brings our stuff in." Her voice trembles and her lip wobbles.

"Waterworks won't work on me, Lys. She's not your servant. Either of you." I fix a stern look on first Alysa and then Mother to convey my point.

"She's not here anyway." Mother brushes off my comment as she turns to speak to Alysa.

"Oh, I forgot," she says, eyes suddenly clear.

"Where is she?" I had expected her to be here when we got back.

Fuck. I've been looking forward to seeing her. It was my reward after a trying afternoon.

"The Christmas tree lighting is tonight. She always goes," Mother explains.

"Why didn't we all go?" I regret the question as soon as I ask.

Mother laughs and places her hand on my arm.

"Channing, dear, why would we?"

To be a part of the community? To enjoy the season? Suggestions for why it would make sense to go push at my lips. Would they do any good? Or would the words be wasted on the two of them? The doubt keeps them locked behind my lips.

"That was always something Mark did with Elle. They always wanted us to come too," Alysa says.

I can picture it. The man in the wedding pictures with Mother, standing next to his daughter who shares his eyes. The two of them earnest in their invitation.

A glance at my watch reads 7:30 p.m.

"What time does the event end?" I ask.

"How should I know?" Mother's response is genuine confusion.

Because you've lived here for years? I almost fire back. Instead I swallow my first response.

"I'm going to head over. I'd like to see it."

The dark tree in the town square the other night—I'll find Elle there.

Mother's apathy is as genuine as it is perplexing.

"Darling, if you've seen one Christmas tree, you've seen them all."

What happened to her?

The woman who raised me had loved Christmas trees, home-made ornaments, and gingerbread houses with drippy frosting. This one didn't even have one decoration up, even though she lived in a town that seemed to plan an entire year's worth of events during the month between Thanksgiving and Christmas.

"Is that why there are no decorations up here?" I ask.

Given how involved in the events Elle seems to be, I would have anticipated the house to be completely decked for the holidays.

"I told Elle three years ago, I refused to put up the tacky decorations she pulled down from the attic."

"So no decorations?"

"What's with the twenty questions? No. It's not like we have any reservations anyway."

"Is that the only reason to have decorations?" Who is this woman?

"What other reason would there be?"

I want to remind her what our Christmases were like growing up—the homemade decorations I brought home from school and the paper snowflakes we made together. But she's already walking toward the house, her bags clutched in her fingers.

Lysa follows, and it's only me left standing behind my open car door with my breath frosting in the air. Breaking through to the two of them is added to my to-do list, but it's not going to be tonight.

Closing the door, I press the button on the fob to lock the car and head toward Main Street in a more direct route than Elle and I took the other night.

The tree is already lit with a rainbow of colors, but people still meander through the square, stopping to visit in clusters.

"Young man!" The sharp voice has me turning my head in its direction.

"Ms. Carter, how are you tonight?"

She harrumphs.

"Getting cold enough to stand in for an icicle waiting on you to show up."

"Me?"

"Did your mother and sister come with you?" she asks,

peering around like we're in the middle of some clandestine conversation.

"Um, no, ma'am. They—"

"Good. Didn't think they would. What's with the ma'am nonsense? We had this talk before. I figured you for someone smarter than to ignore one of his elders."

"Ma—" I start to question but stop when she narrows her eyes. "Fawn."

She smiles.

"Better. Now that that's settled. What are your intentions with our Elle?"

The two other ladies I met on Thanksgiving flank me in a military move a general would be proud of.

"Intentions?"

"Don't dodge the question." She pokes a finger in my direction.

"Good gracious, Fawn. You're scaring him half to death. What she means is we saw a connection between the two of you at Thanksgiving..." Fern says.

"And we heard about the kiss from the Whittakers. They saw you the other night out their front window," Merry adds.

"Do you have feelings for her?" Fawn studies me, crossing her arms while the other two women join her.

Feelings? I have no doubt these three octogenarians would box my ears if I told them my primary feeling involved wanting Elle naked. I cough to clear my throat and buy myself some time to phrase a response that won't get me killed.

"Miss Fawn, what are you three doing? Leave poor Channing alone."

The voice of my salvation interrupts as Elle steps between the three women and me.

"We were having a little chat," Fawn says.

I didn't realize *chat* was another word for interrogation.

"I've heard all about your little chats from Dawn and

Phillip." Elle motions to the couple standing on the edge of our little circle.

"There's no harm in asking," Fawn retorts, but she loses a little steam.

"Channing and I are friends." Elle stresses the last word and I bristle.

Why? It's true.

"Friends don't kiss each other on dark street corners," Merry says.

I cover my laugh with a cough and Elle shoots me a glare.

Fuck, she's cute right now. But I wisely don't add that comment for everyone's consumption.

Elle turns back to the three women with a sigh.

"Miss Fawn, what am I going to do with you?"

"We'll make sure she gets home. Miss Fern and Miss Merry too," Dawn speaks up and her husband groans.

I feel you, man.

"Miss Fawn, did Phillip and I show you the pictures from our honeymoon?" Dawn loops her arm through the older woman's, and Phillip and the other two trail behind them toward the edge of the square.

I can't help but laugh as we watch the party of five move toward a large SUV parked along the street.

She smiles and shakes her head.

"Sorry about them. Since Dawn and Phillip, the three of them now think of themselves as the town matchmakers. They're obsessed with marrying off the rest of my generation and with babies."

The word baby should light a fire under me and send me running for Fiji. But instead I picture Elle holding a baby. One with dark eyes like her mama and a dimple like mine. And I don't hate the image.

Anything but.

"Ready to go?" she asks and I blink, the image vanishing.

"Go?" I glance around and notice the few people left are still working on cleaning up after the event. Most must have left while I was distracted by the Terrifying Trio.

"Unless you have something else you needed to do?" she asks.

"No. I did what I came to do. Find you."

I reach out and lace my fingers with hers and yank her closer.

"You're going to get Fawn, Fern, and Merry going again," she warns.

"Bring them on."

Her smile lights up the dark around us.

Goddamn, she's gorgeous. Without even realizing it. Inside and out.

She falls into step beside me and leans her head against my shoulder. Scents of cool air and cinnamon mix with citrus, and the combination teases my nostrils.

"You smell good," I murmur and tighten my arm around her.

"I doubt it. I probably smell like dust and bleach after deep cleaning the unused guest rooms. I didn't have time to shower before I headed here."

"Is that what you did today?"

"Mmm. Yeah. What about you?"

"Mother and Lysa wanted me to take them to Knoxville."

"The house was definitely quieter."

I bark out a laugh.

"I'm glad one of us had a quiet afternoon."

She giggles and nestles even closer as a breeze kicks up down the street.

"Sorry?"

"Yeah, yeah. I'm glad you got a quieter afternoon, even if I had to deal with them."

We fall into a comfortable silence as we walk, and I enjoy

the weight of her against my arm. But as we turn onto the street where the B&B is located, I know my time with her—unfettered, just the two of us—is limited.

"I've missed you," I tell her.

She stops and her face tilts up and her eyes find mine.

"You hardly know me."

"Is that a requirement to miss someone? How well you know them?"

If so, I should miss Mother and Alysa more. Instead I'm relieved they're not here.

"I-I'm not sure. Maybe?"

"You're saying you didn't miss me?" I ask.

Her cheeks flush pink and she drops her chin.

"I didn't say that," she mumbles.

"I'm sorry. What?" I ask, leaning closer.

"Nothing."

"Nothing?" I lower my arm to her waist and my fingers coast over her side.

She squeals and moves closer to me in an attempt to avoid my fingers.

"Really? Nothing?" I ask.

My smile is inevitable with her breathless giggles.

"Okay, okay. I did," she admits.

I still my fingers, but leave them in place at her waist.

"Did what?"

"I missed you," she says.

"Was that so hard to admit?"

Another breeze kicks up through the street and she shivers, but I still don't want to move.

"A little," she says after a beat. "It's hard to wrap my head around this."

She motions between us.

"What?"

"You're my stepbrother, but..."

"But what?"

Her teeth nibble at her lower lip.

"But what?" I prompt again, using my fingers to lift her chin to meet my gaze.

"We...are what we are...but...there's more."

"More?"

"We had sex. Then the other morning..."

My body hardens in a rush of understanding.

"The other morning we got interrupted," I tell her, stepping closer.

"Yes."

"How did you feel about that?"

I hold my breath and wait for her answer.

"Channing." She groans and tries to pull away but I grip her hands to keep her from running.

"It's a simple question, sweets. Did you enjoy the other morning?"

Her breathing shallows, and her tongue slicks along her lips.

I drop my voice, eliminating the rest of the distance between us.

"Did you enjoy being tongue-fucked on the desk by your stepbrother?"

The moan is almost imperceptible. Almost.

"Do you want more?"

She's silent so long, I question my own perception of her reaction.

"Elle?"

With a deep breath, she squares her shoulders. When her gaze meets mine, an answering fire gives me hope.

"Yes."

"Yes?"

"I want more."

"More of what?" I ask, swallowing around the lust

squeezing my throat.

She lifts on tiptoes to wrap her arms around my neck, the move bringing her breasts flush against my chest. Her lips brush mine teasingly once, twice, before she starts to retreat. My grip on her hips keeps her from going too far.

"I want you, Channing."

"What do you want me to do?" Lust clouds my vision, and I struggle to keep my touch light.

"Kiss me. And don't stop."

CHAPTER 10

Elle

I f I've learned one thing about Channing? I can't predict what he's going to do.

I expect to be thrown over his shoulder caveman style and for him to rush to the inn.

What I don't expect?

For the moment to stretch between us while my demand shimmers in the cool air as the steam from my breath dissipates into nothingness. He closes the distance, and every nerve in my body sits up to reach for him.

"You're sure?" His voice is quiet, husky, and has a direct line to my core.

I nod.

"Yes."

Lifting our joined hands, he presses a hard kiss to the back of my hand and closes the distance a bit more, eliminating another inch of space between us but still not fully connected.

"If I kiss you now and don't stop, we're going to be arrested for public indecency. And that'll really give the ladies something to talk about," he murmurs and one corner of his mouth quirks.

"Maybe we should go back home." This time it's me who moves closer, and I erase the last bit of space between us to press my breasts against his chest.

He sucks in a breath while a muscle pulses in his jaw.

"Maybe we should."

Like some choreographed dance we've practiced hundreds of times before, we move in unison. Our pace isn't slow but it isn't rushed either. I no longer notice the cold around us—I'm surprised by the lack of steam around us given the fire that rages in my body. The way his hand clutches mine, tightening and releasing, his thumb steadily rubbing a soft pattern along my hand, he's right there with me.

The B&B is dark with the exception of the porch light I turned on earlier before I left for the tree lighting. I try to release his hand as we step on the porch and his fingers tighten around mine.

"What are you doing?" he asks.

"What if Trudy or Alysa is awake?"

"So what?"

"How would they feel about this?" I lift our joined hands.

"I don't give a goddamn how they would feel about this. I'm not interested in sneaking around like some little secret, Elle. What they think," he says and lines our bodies up from chest to thigh, "doesn't matter. All that matters is how I feel about you and how you feel about me."

I sink my teeth into my lip to stop from begging him to kiss me again. He lifts his free hand and glides his thumb along the abused flesh until I release it.

"Don't hide from me, sweets. Not anymore. If you have something to say, say it."

"I want you to kiss me."

He groans but the sound doesn't travel far.

"Almost. Keys?"

I hand him my keys, and with a flick of his wrist the door

twists open to a dark—very full—entry where packages are stacked next to the door.

"What the hell?" he hisses.

It isn't the first time I've found the entry full of bags for me to put away. It won't be the last.

"I'll pick them up later."

"The fuck you will. They'll put them away tomorrow. It's not your job."

Unbuttoning my jacket, I pull it off and hang it up before I wrap my arms around him from behind.

"Is this really what you want to focus on now?"

He moves one hand to cover mine where they're joined on his stomach.

"No."

"I believe you promised me something." I move our hands lower and cover the buckle on his belt.

He leaves my hands where they are while he works the top button on his coat. I start with the bottom and we meet in the middle, and I allow my palms the opportunity to glide over the smooth fabric of his sweater.

He shrugs out of his jacket and tosses it in the general direction of the coat rack before spinning to face me.

"You're an instigator."

I lift one shoulder and let it fall.

"You already knew that."

He nods and his eyes darken as he unleashes the fire that burns there.

"You know what happens with instigators?"

"Consequences." I say the word confidently and a shiver works its way down my spine.

"Is that what you're hoping for? Consequences?" He reaches out a hand, one finger gliding along my jaw in a charged caress.

Closing my eyes, I lean into the touch.

"Mmm."

"Not an answer, sweets."

Blinking my eyes open, I meet his gaze.

"Consequences or not, I'm still waiting for my kiss."

He leans down, his lips covering mine and his tongue immediately pressing forward to find mine.

I twine my fingers in his hair, holding him in place and sinking into the kiss that only drives the need for him higher. I protest when he breaks the kiss, my quiet cry turning into a squeal as he swoops me bridal style into his arms.

"What are you doing?" I ask.

He nips another chaste kiss and takes the stairs two at a time while managing to avoid the squeaky spots—something that took me years of practice to learn.

"How...?"

"I'm a quick study," he whispers.

The din of the TV comes from Trudy's room as we creep by and there's a light under Alysa's door, but he doesn't hesitate to move to his bedroom door, opening and closing it behind us with a quiet snick of the lock.

"I have something for you," he tells me.

He releases my knees and I slide down his body. His erection creates a delicious friction and I lean toward him.

"I just bet you do," I tease.

He chuckles.

"That too, sweets. But that's not what I was talking about."

He walks past me into the bathroom and rummages in a bag on the counter before he turns out the light and steps back into the bedroom. His facial expression is a mix of emotions—the desire still burning in his eyes, the softening of his lips as he studies me, the tick of his jaw as he closes the distance.

"What?" I ask.

"Close your eyes."

I lift one brow but he waits until I give in and let my lids fall shut. All my other senses tune to his movements, his presence as he shifts around me. So close his breath stirs the hair near my ears in a tickling caress.

"Shift your hair to one side."

The vibration of the words is more obvious than the volume, and I shiver as goose bumps line my spine. But I do as he says.

"Channing?"

"No peeking."

My breathing quickens as I wait, my heart rate picking up speed as my awareness of him continues to build to almost unbearable levels. I want him to touch me. I'm more than ready for it. So what is he waiting for?

His fingers brush my neck but are gone before I can lean against them. At the slight weight that settles against my chest, my eyes fly open and my fingers move to the familiar shape I had missed for a month.

"My necklace?" I spin around, still clutching one of the few pieces of my mother I have left, and tears burn behind my eyes.

"You left it behind."

"I..." I swallow around the lump of emotion in my throat. "I called the hotel, but no one found it."

His grin is sheepish.

"I probably should have left it with them. But it was the only proof I had our night was real. That you were real. Without it, I felt like maybe I imagined the whole thing."

Maybe I should be upset he didn't turn the necklace over. But maybe it was fate he kept it. Maybe it was the same way I felt when I lifted the shirt I had worn from his hotel room that morning and it still held traces of his cologne.

"You probably want your shirt back," I tell him.

He flexes a hand on either of my hips and hauls me closer to him.

"You can keep it. I know you're real now."

He lifts slightly while he dips down, crashing his lips to mine. Twining my arms around his neck, I deepen the kiss and slide my fingers through the smooth strands of his hair to hold him to me. His tongue tangles with mine as he walks us backward to the bed, sitting down on the mattress and pulling me between his legs. With our height difference, I don't have to bend very far to maintain the connection.

His hands slide to my backside, squeezing my flesh through the denim. I want the sensation of skin against skin, and my fingers fumble on the button of my jeans before I'm able to rip them open and shimmy them down my hips. Now the only thing separating us is the thin layer of my panties, but even that's too much. He must think so too, because his hands delve beneath the elastic to grip the skin beneath.

I continue to shake loose of my jeans and kick my shoes off to free myself completely of them before I advance. He leans back and I move with him, straddling him on the bed and rubbing along his erection.

I break the kiss on a moan, and he hisses out a breath.

"Fuck," he growls and squeezes my ass roughly to rub me faster against him.

How is it that an orgasm shimmers along the edges and we're only dry humping like teenagers?

"Too. Many. Clothes." My breath comes in pants, and the few things I'm still wearing weigh me down.

"I can fix that." He shifts quickly, rolling us on the bed and lifting off in an almost seamless blur of motion and strength.

His sweater is first to come off and be tossed in the corner, and his T-shirt quickly follows. A light dusting of hair covers his chest, and my palms tingle with the need to catalog the contrast between rough hair and smooth, warm skin. Toeing out of his shoes, he kicks them to the side and lifts his hands to the buckle on his belt, opening it, and pausing.

"I promised myself I wouldn't rush this," he tells me and closes the distance between us.

"You did?"

He nods and sinks into a crouch at my feet.

"You're not a quick fuck, Elle. It may have started as a one-night stand—we may have started that way—but that's not what I want."

He lifts his hands to cup my knees, his thumbs rubbing along the inside. I'm not sure if it's his touch or his words that have more of an impact in the moment.

"You don't?"

The corner of his mouth lifts in a smirk.

"Don't get me wrong. I want you more than I want my next breath. But I want more."

"What does that mean? More?"

Why are you questioning what you already know?

My heart may already be on the same page, but I need him to spell out what he means with that word. For all I know, maybe he's only looking for a standing hookup when he's in town.

"More. Holiday events like tonight where I'm by your side, quiet walks with hot chocolate from Mistletoe Café, stealing kisses on dark street corners. I'm falling for you, Elle. And it would be so easy to love you. To let myself fall for you. I'm not in this alone, am I?"

I shake my head and grip his hand to pull him closer, and we both tumble back to the bed.

"You're not. Since our night in Nashville we've had this connection. One that reminds me of my parents. One I always wanted to find for myself."

His mouth finds mine, moving slowly, worshipping every

small centimeter until my legs are locked around his waist to hold him to me.

He breaks the kiss and his lips find the pulse point in my throat.

"Are you ready for more, sweets?"

He looks up, his eyes locking with mine in an unspoken connection. One that's more than lust.

"I'm ready for it all," I tell him. "I'm ready for everything."

CHAPTER 11

Elle

He shifts back, bringing me with him until we're sitting up, then grabs the hem of my sweater.

His fingers flutter along the sensitive skin and almost tickle, but the sensation is more an electric current than a light touch, and I nod.

"Yes."

I lift my arms and help him rid me of my sweater inch by teasing inch. His fingertips drag a light line as they move up, and I'm left in just my bra and panties. I bend my arms back, my fingers finding the clasp of my bra.

"Let me?"

My fingers drop at his husky question and I nod. His hands find the clasp and twist, then he pulls the bra off as his hands retreat. My nipples pebble with the mix of cool air, and his focus drops to my chest, tightening them further.

He closes his eyes on a groan, dropping one of his hands to his denim-clad erection and squeezing roughly.

I hook my fingers in the loops at his waist and his eyes pop back open. His entire body is tense, a rubber band on the verge of snapping, and his hands hold a slight tremor when he lifts one to my cheek.

"Do you know how badly I want you?"

His thumb sweeps my cheekbone in a gentle caress.

"As much as I want you?"

His lips crash to mine again, his tongue plundering my mouth, and my hands push under his shirt, finishing the job of undoing his fly before pushing under his jeans to push them and his boxers off his hips. Between the two of us, we manage to shove them off. His erection stretches toward me and heat floods my core.

One of his arms bands behind my back and yanks me to him while the other finds the waistband of my panties to push them off. Only once we're both completely naked does he lay us back on the bed, his mouth pressing hot kisses down my neck and collarbone.

"Please," I beg but I'm unsure where I want his touch next.

His kisses drop to my breasts, his tongue circling my nipple before he drags it into his mouth and sucks hard. Using lips, tongue, and teeth, he creates a needy ache between my legs, and my hips shift against the bed, seeking a friction just out of reach. The sharp nip of his teeth on my breast is an electric current flashing through my body. I jump and press myself closer to his mouth while my other breast receives the tugging attention of his fingers.

He releases the suction of his mouth with a pop and switches to the other, laving the tip with the flat of his tongue before tracing the shape. His fingers pinch the other tip, and he twists at the same time he bites down.

I mewl, my thighs pressing against both of his hips. His dick slides through my folds, brushing against my clit, and I shift to try and move him where I ache for him most.

"Patience," he tells me and moves down to press light kisses on the underside of my breasts.

Now both of his hands cover my breasts, and I cover them with my own. Hot, open-mouthed kisses shift lower, down my abdomen until he can tongue my navel. I squirm, and his warm breath washes against my lower abdomen with his chuckle.

"I love how responsive you are," he murmurs.

"Only with you."

He lifts his gaze to mine with my admission, and the heat visible in his eyes flares and creates a response in the fire currently consuming me. The moment stretches between us, neither of us moving, as we communicate without words. I'm not sure if the need is greater because of the emotion or if the emotion builds with the need. Maybe it's a chicken or the egg debate, but I don't care. All that matters is the two of us in this moment.

I suck in a breath, and my entire body revels in the weight of him where he presses between my legs and where his hands cup my breasts. My first response is to make a smart-ass quip to ease the overwhelming sensations swamping me. To ease some of the sexual tension that simmers in the air like a tangible thing in the room with us.

It's on the tip of my tongue when he finally moves, dropping his head to trace kisses along the crease of my thigh before he tugs his hands free and presses my legs up and back. The heat of his attention on my pussy is enough to make my hips shift restlessly along the bed, seeking the promise of pleasure he's more than capable of delivering.

He doesn't make me wait long, dragging his tongue in a smooth line from back to front, circling my clit before tapping the hard bundle of nerves. My hands tighten on my breasts, and I bite my lip to avoid crying out, muffling myself to a moan.

"I want to hear you, sweets," he tells me before repeating the caress, dueling his tongue with my clit until stars dance behind my eyelids.

My breathing stalls, and I release the hold on my lips in an attempt to drag oxygen into my body. Closing his lips around the hard bundle, his cheeks hollow with the suction of his mouth and I cry out. The stars in my vision grow brighter as I rocket closer to them, the orgasm pushing me faster to the edge.

"*Channing.*"

The edges of his teeth are sharp, bringing the pleasure to the line of pleasure and pain.

"Oh my god." I struggle to get the words out, but need some way to channel the intensity overwhelming me.

"Come for me, Elle," he growls and repeats the caress.

Once. Twice. Until I break apart into a million pieces of stardust and light, anchored to earth only by the man whose name breaks on my lips. It's a blinding white flash of light and heat where sensations blur in lightning arcs of pleasure until I slowly come back to reality and flutter my eyes open.

Channing studies me, a foil packet gripped between two of his fingers, and I reach up and snatch it from him.

"May I?"

"Whatever you want, Elle. If it's in my power to give it to you, it's yours."

His muscles lock, but as my fingers brush the tip of his cock, the muscle in his jaw jumps and he sucks a breath in through his teeth.

"Fuck," he groans.

Gripping the foil packet in my teeth is impossible as my lips tilt into a smile and I grab the packet before it can drop.

"Hurry up."

"What was it you told me earlier? Patience?" I tease.

He snatches the condom from me to rip it open and slide

it over his dick with hurried movements. With that done, he lunges toward me, trapping me under him on the bed, and I squeal.

"There's time for patience. Later," he says.

I open my mouth to respond, but he fuses his lips to mine and our tongues tangle together. He lines the head of his dick at my entrance and pushes forward an inch. I moan and wiggle my hips to try and move closer.

"Do you feel me, sweets? I'm right here."

Another inch and the delicious stretch I remember filters through my blood and fills my body. An orgasm beckons and moves closer and I lift my hips, frustrated when he stops moving.

"Please," I beg. I grip his shoulders, my fingertips pricking into the skin.

His hips pulse once and he grits his teeth.

"If you keep doing that, I'm not going to last."

"I'm close," I tell him. "Please."

The dark brown of his irises is practically black and eclipsed by the heat that engulfs the two of us.

"Hold on to me."

"I am." I flex my hands to prove my point.

"Don't let go."

"I—"

He pulls back and almost pulls out completely before slamming forward in one sharp thrust.

"Don't let go."

"I won't."

He retreats and snaps forward again until his hips bump mine. Slowly he starts to move, building speed as he continues to drive us both to the pinnacle we know is waiting for us. Over and over again until sweat slicks our skin and my hands slip along his shoulders. His lips find my jaw, and he traces the line with his tongue until he reaches my ear.

"Hold on, sweets."

His pace increases, and the force of the orgasm building curls my toes. I keep my grip, lifting my hips to meet his. His rhythm falters, but he quickly recovers, bracketing my hips with his hands and holding me in place while he drives in and out, and yanks me to him as he drives toward me.

"Oh god."

"Are you close?"

"Mmm," I moan, trying to nod.

"Tell me," he demands.

"I'm so close." The words are a combination of a moan and a pant.

His pelvis hits mine again, and he holds me to him, spinning us until I straddle him in the bed.

"Open your eyes," he says and weaves our fingers together.

Blinking my eyes open, I can't look away from him. We're locked in some game, neither of us willing to break the contact, despite how powerful the orgasm is, tightening all the muscles of my legs as it builds.

"Fuck, that's right, baby. Squeeze my cock with your pussy."

Every movement of my body is under his control, and all of my concentration is centered on the waves of pleasure as they wash through me, lapping at my feet and up my legs faster than I can fully catalog before they crest over me. Even as the heat overtakes my vision, I can't look away, locked in the center of his attention. He releases whatever hold he held over his control, and his hips push forward, pistoning in powerful strokes until the tendons on his neck stand in relief, his own orgasm pouring from him in a loud groan.

He pulls me onto his chest, and my cheek finds the steady thud of his heartbeat while his hands sweep over my back.

"I don't think I can move," I murmur and press my lips against his chest.

"I wouldn't let you go even if you tried. You're mine now, Elle."

His. A shiver works itself down my spine.

My heartbeat aligns to his, and the warm drag of his fingers across my back relaxes me further.

"Yours," I repeat and snuggle closer into his embrace.

The pressure of his lips finds the top of my head and he releases a sigh.

"I'm so happy," he whispers and my heart melts.

Happily ever after.

Maybe it's time it came true?

CHAPTER 12

Channing

The angry vibration of my phone dragging against the wooden nightstand pulls me from a peaceful—and much needed—sleep. Elle shifts against me, her ass brushing against my dick and taking me from a semi to ready for another opportunity to bury itself in her pussy. Three? Four? Several times in the middle of the night we turned toward each other, so the fact that my phone is ringing while it's still dark outside is bullshit.

I have no desire to let go of the beauty sleeping in my arms to roll over and grab my phone.

I'll check who it was later.

Elle shifts again.

"What was that?" she murmurs.

I tighten my arm to hold her in place when she starts to roll away.

"Phone call. I'll check later."

"I should get up and go to my room."

Despite my protests, Elle has kept our relationship hidden from Mother and Alysa. She doesn't want to make her life more difficult, and while I can't understand her line of reasoning, I am respecting her decision. For now.

But I am sick of sneaking around. Of her double-checking before she kisses me in the kitchen. Of the clandestine meetings in my room every night when Mother and Alysa are in their rooms, either asleep or occupied with something else.

"Not yet," I grumble and drag her closer to me.

She snuggles closer, her hand coming up to rest on my arm locked around her waist.

"I need to get up soon."

"Why?"

"Breakfast."

"There's no one here but us."

She cranes her head over her shoulder.

"And your mom and Alysa."

"Who will both sleep in." I press a kiss to her forehead and take note of the dark circles under her eyes. "Get some more rest."

"But—"

"But nothing. Sleep. If Mom or Lys wakes up, I'll take care of it."

She turns her head, rubbing her cheek against the pillow, and lets out a sigh as her body relaxes again.

"Just a little more sleep. Can you set your alarm for an hour?"

"Okay."

I wait until her breaths are deep and even before I reluctantly let her go to grab my phone to set the alarm.

Missed Call.

Why was Hayden calling me when he knew the time difference between where he is and I am? Maybe the text he sent will clear things up.

HAYDEN

Need you to call me. ASAP.

Fuck.

Easing my way from the bed, I grab pajama pants and a T-shirt before opening and closing the bedroom door without a sound. The grandfather clock in the lobby shows it's nearly five, so whatever reason he has for calling me must be important.

I forgo the kitchen and head into the office and take a seat at a desk much more cluttered than it was when I arrived. Elle and I have been poring over information trying to figure out why her reservations have disappeared completely.

Once situated, I click on Hayden's contact and bring the phone to my ear.

"Finally."

"That's one hell of a greeting. Do you remember the time difference here?"

"Couldn't be helped. You need to get here now. Like yesterday."

I scrub a hand down my face and struggle to keep myself awake.

"What?"

"I can't do this on my own anymore, Chan. I'm calling in reinforcements."

"Fuck, how bad is it?"

"The owner told me I can stay through the weekend, but he's signing papers with the developers. He's selling to them."

"Shit. When is he supposed to finalize the paperwork with them?"

I switch to speakerphone and pull up a search to find a

flight. A last-minute flight is going to cost a shit ton, but hopefully I can convince the owner not to sell.

"Tomorrow."

"Tomorrow?! I can't even book a flight out until this afternoon. I need you to stall him."

"Stall him? How the fuck am I supposed to do that when nothing I've done has worked so far?"

"Ask him, dumbass. Let him know I'm on my way and I'd like to meet with him before he signs anything."

"You think that'll work?"

"It's worth a shot. I'm booking my flight now and will text you the info so you can relay it. I want you to send me any notes or other info you have on the place while you've been on site."

"On their way to you...now."

My phone pings with the receipt of the email.

"Okay, I'll take a look at this and send you anything I can think of as I review."

"And you'll send me flight information."

"Yes."

"See you soon," he says, and the smile in his voice is obvious.

"Yeah, yeah. Don't sound so happy about it."

I hang up on his laughter and pull up the email on my phone.

Hayden is a great business partner. The way he can look at numbers is practically magical. But the small-ass sized print for all of his notes is enough to give me the impression I'm going blind.

"Fuck this," I mumble to myself and turn to the ancient desktop sitting on the desk beside me.

I've watched Elle turn it on a few times and am used to the god-awful speed it takes to fully power on with the familiar chime of the operating system bringing back high school nostalgia. I count my lucky stars the damn thing has wireless and not dial-up and load my mail service on the Internet and open Hayden's email again.

"Better."

But not by much. Regardless, I review the pages once for the overall picture before scrolling to the top of the document. Grabbing a pad of paper and pen from the desk, I review each of Hayden's notes methodically, cataloging suggestions and points I'd like to make to the owner.

By the end of the first page of his notes, I've filled four pages of my own notes and scrub my eyes as I squint and continue to read.

Beach is pristine, but very few amenities.

Closing my eyes, I pull up images of my last trip. Hayden and I had popped over from Australia as our last project was winding down, a long weekend once we heard of the hotel where Hayden is now. A friend of the owner's had recommended us, and his email had invited us to come see what paradise was.

He wasn't lying.

It had been hard to concentrate and too easy to relax on the beach.

Maybe it is time for a vacation. Or at least once I fix the current mess.

I could take Elle to Canberra Bells in Australia and show her what we did with that hotel. Laze on the beach and enjoy her in a bright-pink barely there bikini.

No.

Turquoise.

It matches the water as she wades in, sighing as the luke-warm water kisses her thighs.

"Come here."

She crooks a finger, beckoning me from my beach chair

where I've pretended to go to sleep. My eyes—trained on her—are hidden behind dark sunglasses.

"Are you wearing sunscreen?"

Her lips quirk in a mischievous smile.

"Maybe you better come find out." Her finger beckons again.

The sun is warm as I shift lazily, coming to my feet and trailing her into the water. Reaching up my hand, I grip the messy bun and angle her mouth toward mine.

"Welcome to paradise, sweets."

"Mmm." Her eyes flutter shut and her lips open as she tilts her head back to invite my kiss.

Don't mind if I do.

Once. Twice. A languid dance of tongues as we enjoy the quiet beach.

Her and me.

Happily ever after.

CHAPTER 13

Elle

T he clearing of a throat has me bolting upright.

Because it's not Channing's deep timbre.

It's one rife with disgust and judgment. A tone I know well.

Trudy.

"What are *you* doing in *here*?" She sneers as I yank the covers over my nakedness.

"Where's Channing?"

I remember telling him to set the alarm specifically to avoid a situation like this.

"My son's whereabouts are none of your concern."

The fuck they aren't.

It's hard to swallow the retort, but I manage at the last minute.

"Is this the type of behavior that has dried up reservations? I didn't realize the bed and breakfast we were running could double as a brothel. What would your father say?"

Those words are it. The snapping point I've needed for three long years of trying to keep the peace. Of stuffing my pride down to keep some connection to my parents by keeping the inn they loved running.

My parents taught me to defend myself and those too weak to help themselves. They taught me to love this place, this town. And myself.

Tugging the sheet with me to wrap it around me, I stand up.

"What would my father say? Trudy, how the hell would you know what my dad would have to say? I'll tell you since you obviously have no idea who he was despite being married to him for five years."

Her eyes widen and she steps back despite the fact that I haven't moved other than to stand from the bed.

"My parents taught me a lot of things. Love was only one of them. Loving this place, meeting new people, introducing them to this town and the surrounding areas. Loving our close-knit community and helping neighbors when you could and celebrating when the occasion called for it. They are not beneath you despite your snide comments through the years. We are not less than you just because you think you're better than everyone else."

"How—"

I continue as if she hasn't tried to speak.

"Something else my parents taught me about love. It was when you find it, you hang on to it. You let yourself feel it. Because life is too short to walk away from it."

"You're saying you *love* my son?"

I do. Even though right now I want to strangle him. I'm pissed as hell he's not here to help handle his mother.

Had he woken me up on time, I wouldn't have to.

But maybe the time for hiding is done. From her. From how I feel about him.

"That is none of your business, Trudy. Nothing between the two of us is."

"What do you think the town will have to say? You caught with your *stepbrother*?"

Fawn, Fern, and Merry come to mind. Something tells me the town would be more than okay with Channing and me being together, regardless of the stepsibling relationship. But nothing I say is going to make a difference with her.

"If you have to ask, you really don't know anybody in this town as well as you think you do."

I take two steps toward the door and she reaches out, yanking me around to face her.

"I'm not finished talking to you."

"I have nothing else to say to you."

"You really think Channing is in love with you? That he's serious about you? The *help*? You're a convenient distraction while he's here. Nothing more. Did he tell you why he was here?" The smile on her face is cold, calculating, and sends a shiver down my spine.

For the first time since this conversation started, my confidence wavers.

"To help identify ways to update the hotel."

"Why?"

Her fingers curl around my bicep, her long nails digging into the soft skin at the back of my arm.

"To increase reservations." Wasn't it? He hadn't explicitly said it, but why else would he be here?

Trudy shakes her head at me, her eyes tilting into an expression of pity.

"You poor, sweet child. He didn't tell you, did he?"

Her pity is more than I can take.

"What is it he supposedly didn't tell me?" I bite out the words.

"I'm selling the inn. With his advice. And I'll be using the money to move Alysa and me back to Nashville where we

129

belong. There's a realtor coming day after tomorrow to initiate the paperwork and listing."

The news settles in my stomach like a giant boulder, and the sting of tears builds behind my nose. But I'll be damned if I give her the reaction she's looking for. Deep down, I had a suspicion she wanted to sell the B&B. That the last connection to my parents was fading. I had hoped to be able to afford to buy it from her someday.

It looks like my time is up. Which makes what I want to do so much easier.

"And in case it wasn't clear, you're fired. I expect you gone by the end of the day."

I shake loose of her grip and reach for the door handle.

"There's no need to fire me, Trudy. I quit. And I'll be gone within the hour."

She doesn't follow me, which I'm grateful for since I don't know how much fight I have left in me. As for Channing and his disappearing act, I'll figure that out later.

"Dad, what were you thinking?" Leaning against the door, I lift my hand and toy with the ring, needing the small connection.

Was it the simple fact he never updated his will after Mom passed? That the inn was written to go to his spouse who just happened to be Trudy?

Grief swamps me. I've lost Mom, then Dad, and now this place. But I've also lost something else. Something I hadn't planned on.

I've lost my heart.

I want more.

Was it just a line he fed me to convince me to sleep with him again? Was I really just a convenient distraction?

My heart says no. He had no reason to lie to me.

But he didn't tell you why he was really here.

There has to be some explanation.

But when I need him to explain it he's disappeared. Where is he?

Swiping at the unwelcome tears, I take a deep breath.

"This isn't getting you anywhere," I tell myself.

I need to pack. I'd already put some stuff in storage when I moved from Knoxville—pictures and keepsakes from Mom I had in my apartment. I have a few other boxes in my room of things that remind me of Dad, keeping them there after Trudy tried to donate them last year.

Throwing on jeans and a sweater, I tug my suitcase from under the bed and toss it on the lumpy twin mattress. I don't try to organize any of what I toss in my suitcase and the half-empty box, and the only thing left is the blue silk dress from Halloween I'd hung in the back of my closet as a reminder of that night. I glide my hands along the cool fabric, and it slips through my fingers like water.

"I don't really need you, though, do I?" I ask and scoff. "Great, now I'm talking to inanimate objects."

The last of the fabric glides along my fingers, and I step back and close the door. I'm not the same woman I was when I donned that dress. I'm not even the same one who hid it in the back of my closet.

I am done hiding behind masks. I am done hiding who I am.

"Do you want another latte, hon?" Dina steps out from behind the counter and moves closer to me after her morning rush.

I've been sitting at a table in Mistletoe Café, my car filled with my suitcase and three boxes parked behind town square. The plan when I got here was to eat something and figure out my next move.

I don't want to leave Mistletoe Creek. This place is my home. Dina, Missy, Fern, Fawn, Merry. And everyone else. These people are my family.

But I don't want to stay at Mistletoe Lodge at the edge of town. The place is dirty and the manager way too sketchy for my liking. I texted Posey earlier, but haven't heard from her yet. I'm sure she'll let me stay with her in Charlotte. But I don't relish the thought of that drive at this time of year.

The bells above the door jangle and Merry bustles in, shivering dramatically.

"Cold as a frosted frog out there."

I giggle at her words, the first smile or laugh I've had all morning.

Her responding smile is broad, and she approaches Dina and me at the table.

"Miss Merry, you here for your monthly order?" Dina asks.

Merry nods.

"My turn to pick up the cookies for our po...bridge game."

I use my hand to cover my broadening smile.

Dad had shared once that the ladies play a monthly poker game, but the entire town thinks they play bridge. I have no idea how he found out, but I have kept the secret.

"Two dozen snickerdoodles and a dozen oatmeal scotchies." Dina nods and heads into the back.

Merry turns to me. "It's a bit early for you to be out and about, isn't it, Elle? You're normally elbow deep in breakfast clean-up."

I lift my cup to my mouth without realizing it's empty. With a grimace I set it back down.

"I...uh...well, I guess news travels fast so I might as well tell you. Trudy is selling the bed and breakfast. And I quit this morning."

She doesn't seem surprised, her facial expression morphing to one of pride.

"Good girl! We've been waiting for this for a long time."

"We?"

"Fern, Fawn, and I. Fawn thought you were going to quit the first year after your dad passed. Fern had you into next year, but I had you down for somewhere in the middle."

"Down?"

"We had a little wager going on."

Of course they did.

"What?"

She waves at Dina who stands behind the counter with three small pastry boxes.

"I'll be right there, Dina. But maybe you could bring me a tea?"

"Miss Merry, what's going on?" I ask.

She waits until Dina brings the small ceramic cup and teapot, then doctors a cup of tea before answering my question.

"We always knew Trudy wasn't right for your daddy. Watching him and your mama, anyone could tell they were soulmates. Meant to be. And then you came along and y'all were the perfect little family. You were a spitfire from day one. Running all over town with Persephone Turner."

Her smile is distracted, her eyes focused on her memory as she takes a sip of her drink.

"Miss Merry?"

She blinks and refocuses on me, the edges of her smile tipped down in a sad version of her previous one.

"When your mama passed, we all mourned. It was hard to lose someone so young. Someone so...loved."

Tears line my lashes, and I wipe them away while she does the same.

"But when Mark brought home Trudy, we had hope.

Here she was with a sister for you, and we expected her to be like your mama. Turns out we were all wrong, even if Trudy managed to fool your daddy as long as she did. As soon as he wasn't looking, we all saw the real her. Then to lose him too..."

I'd been so busy in Knoxville, I hadn't been around to witness what she was talking about. Trudy and Alysa were there, but peripherally, in my memories with Dad.

"But how can Trudy sell the inn? Doesn't it belong to you?"

"Belong to me?"

"Your daddy mentioned once he was meeting with Gepetto to update his will. He wanted to make sure you were taken care of."

Oh, Dad.

"According to Trudy, he left the inn to her."

"Did you ever confirm that?"

"Well, no. You're saying she lied?"

"I'm saying I'd want to look into it, if I were you." She lifts an eyebrow and takes another drink.

"I'll have to figure it out once I find a place to stay."

"Stay?"

"I moved out."

"I assumed so, but why is that a question?"

"Where else would I go?"

"The question, little Elle, isn't where else you would go."

"It's not?"

"It's where you'll go."

"Where will I go?"

"It's funny you should ask. It just so happens I have a guest room."

She stands and gestures for me to join her.

"Grab the cookies, sweetie. Let's get you settled. Have you ever played bridge?"

"Bridge?"
"We'll teach you."

CHAPTER 14

Channing

The slamming of a door wakes me, and I immediately reach for my neck, rubbing at the crick there after falling asleep in the chair.

"Shit! What time is it?"

Grabbing my phone, I nearly drop it.

"Fuck. I have to be at the airport in four hours!"

It'll take three to drive to Nashville, two and a half if I'm lucky.

Rushing out of the office, I nearly run over Alysa on her way into the kitchen.

"Watch it."

"Sorry."

"Channing, there you are." Mother turns from the stairs toward the two of us.

"Yes, but not for long. I need to be at the airport and head to Fiji."

"Fiji?" She wrinkles her nose as if she doesn't understand.

"We have a project about to fall through."

"Very well."

"Have you—"

Shit, Elle. I was supposed to set an alarm and wake her up. I bolt for the stairs and take them two at a time to my room only to find it empty.

"Have you seen Elle?" I yell, coming back downstairs.

"Elle?" Mother asks.

"She took her tacky wardrobe and left," Alysa mumbles.

"What?"

"I saw her loading some boxes and her suitcase into her car."

"What? Why?"

"Who knows? Who cares?" Alysa snorts.

"Mother?"

"She quit this morning. Rather unexpectedly."

Shit.

"Why?"

"She didn't say. But that brings up something I wanted to speak to you about. Really, Channing?"

"Really, what?"

"She's the help."

"She's more than the help."

"She's your stepsister."

"Who the fuck cares?"

"I do!" Mother raises her voice, her expression twisting to one of anger. Her lips are pursed, her eyebrows furrowed as her nose wrinkles.

"What?"

"You could do so much better."

"She's who I want."

Who I love.

But I'm not going to tell Mother and Alysa before I have the chance to tell her. And apologize for not waking her up.

Something tells me her wake-up had been ruder than mine.

"Where is she?" I repeat.

"She didn't say."

"Now we can enjoy Christmas just the three of us. Like it was before," Alysa says. There's an undercurrent to her tone, and I ignore Elle's whereabouts for the moment.

"Why do you say that?"

"I'm tired of sharing my house at Christmas. I wanted to have a Christmas like we used to. Just the family."

"What did you do, Lys?"

She shrugs.

"I canceled the reservations that were booked. And changed the website listing for the inn as unavailable for the entire month."

"Alysa!" Mother's surprise is genuine so at least she wasn't in on it.

My sister shrugs again.

"I don't see what the big deal is."

"Big deal? Alysa, the inn only stays open because of reservations," I tell her.

"Mother wants to sell it anyway."

It's like I'm at a tennis match, splitting my attention between these two.

"Is that why you invited me here? To help you sell it?"

"Yes."

"Mother, I came to give you advice on whether you *should* sell it or not. Which I don't think you should."

"It's too late. I have a realtor coming in a few days to list it."

"What? Does Elle know?" I ask.

"I told her this morning."

That explains why she quit.

Fuck.

My phone pings with the notification to check in for my flight.

I'll have to deal with all of this from the airport. And track

Elle down as best I can until I can wrap up Fiji and head back here.

"I have to go."

"Of course, darling. Work comes first."

God, her priorities are so screwed up. Regardless, she and Alysa are still my family, and I give them both a quick hug.

"I'm going to go pack."

I'm nearly to the stairs when a question pops into my head.

"Lys, how did you make all those changes?"

She rolls her eyes. "Duh. It's not like the accounts were locked when I turned on the behemoth in there."

She thumbs toward the office.

Noted. Change passwords. Or advise Elle to once I can find her.

My phone pings again reminding me time is running out.

Shit.

"We're not done with this conversation," I tell the two of them.

They both look at each other and neither responds. I don't have the time to wait for one.

I have to fix one mess before I can fix this.

If there's anything left to fix after this morning.

"Would you please quit looking like somebody kicked your fucking dog?" Hayden wads up a paper from the top of the stack and throws it at me.

I bat it away before it connects with my head and flip him the bird.

"Come on, man. Cheer up. You managed to save this project and we start after the new year. Based on all the ideas you presented earlier, I thought you'd be more excited we won."

"Won?"

"We did it. We beat the developers this time."

It hadn't taken much. But it did require a human touch Hayden didn't possess. An ability to connect with the owner on an emotional level.

The owner thought of this place like Elle thought of hers.

And it took her to teach me what that felt like.

"Yeah. We did."

And the one person I wanted to share it with had disappeared. Not really. Not like before.

But I don't have her cell number. I don't have an email address. And emailing the inn is out. Especially since Alysa can access it. I hadn't had time to try to track her down after I packed. Fuck, I had almost missed the check-in time I needed for my flight.

"Elle?" he asks.

My best friend guesses it in one, and I nod.

"Any word?"

"How? It's not like I gave her my cell phone number."

There hadn't been a need to share cell phone numbers when we lived under the same roof and she shared my bed.

"Who does that?" Hayden asks.

"Why did I need it? If I wanted to talk to her I could track her down in the house."

"Um, hello? What about sexting? Dirty pics?"

"No."

"No? Never?" His eyes widen like I just told him I am a virgin.

I groan.

"Not never. But it's not something I do all the time."

"It's not a bad way to end the night after a hard day's work."

"When was the last time you worked hard?"

"Fucker." This time it's his turn to flip me off.

"Couldn't resist." The corner of my lips lift in a half smile.

"Well, quit giving me shit and fix your fucking life."

"How?"

"What the fuck? Do I have to do every fucking thing for you?"

"What do you mean?"

He rolls his eyes and motions for my phone until I hand it over.

"First things first..." He spends several moments in silence while his fingers fly over the phone.

"What are you doing?"

"Buying you another plane ticket....and done."

"For Nashville?"

"No, for Antarctica. Yes, for Nashville."

"She probably hates me," I tell him.

Why else would she leave the inn without talking to me?

Hey, moron, it's not like she knew where you were. You left her in your *bed, not the other way around.*

"Boo fucking hoo. I've never known you to sound so pathetic over a girl."

"I've never felt this way before."

It's as close as I'm going to come to admitting my feelings for her. She's going to be the first one I tell. Once I find her.

"So how are you going to fix it then?"

Good question.

"I need to figure out this realtor bullshit my mom sprang on me before I left."

"Is it weird her dad left the inn completely to your mom, or is it just me?" he asks after several minutes of silence.

"I still can't figure that out."

"Well, did you check the state to see if his will was filed?"

"Do they do that?"

He shrugs. "Sometimes. Every state has different laws."

Grabbing my laptop, I open a browser window and do a search for Tennessee will laws.

"Wills have to be filed with the state in Tennessee."

"So what does her dad's say?"

I read through the rest of the page and click on the link for the request.

"I have to send in a request."

"So do it."

"What do you think I'm doing?" I fire back, filling out the few boxes and clicking submit at the bottom of the page.

"So you're looking into that, and I booked you a plane ticket. What about Elle?"

"I don't know where she is!"

Maybe she doesn't want me to come back.

"Oh, gee, it's too bad she doesn't live in a town that catalogs all their holiday activities as part of their tourism package."

"Well...fuck, why didn't I think of that?"

"What would you do without me?"

He pulls the laptop closer to him and pulls up the web page for Mistletoe Creek.

There's a listing of the holiday events for the season and different pictures from the ones that have already happened. One stands out from a post updated yesterday.

"Christmas Light Fight winner announced. Let's hear it for Paul Whittaker for his second win in a row," Hayden reads. The picture is of the winner receiving the prize of a massive, tangled ball of Christmas lights reminiscent of *National Lampoon's Christmas Vacation*.

In the side of the image, with her arm looped with Merry and a giant smile on her face?

Elle.

"The picture was from a few days ago. Looks like you know where she is."

"Yep."

"You have any idea what you're going to say to her?"

"Nope. But I've got a long-ass plane ride to figure it out."

And I'm not going to stop until I've done two things.

I'm going to tell Elle Thompson I'm in love with her.

And I'm going to fight like hell to be with her.

CHAPTER 15

Elle

The last week had been a roller-coaster ride of ups and downs.

It was overwhelming to me how much the town had supported me after news traveled. I think the realtor was still hammering in the for sale sign in my front yard when the news filtered through the grapevine.

My *former* front yard.

The place I had called home for my entire life, a connection with my parents, is now on the market for whomever wants it.

I am homeless.

Despite being offered an indefinite invitation to stay with Miss Merry. Regardless of the demands I had from Posey to come stay with her.

My home is gone.

"Did you hear the news?" Dawn slides up to me at the hot chocolate table at the Breakfast with Santa we're both working and distracts me from my morose thoughts.

The giggles of the children waiting for the jolly man himself filter back in, and I blink to bring her back into focus.

"What news?"

"There's a realtor and potential buyers at the inn today."

I nearly fumble the cup of hot chocolate I've been sipping from absentmindedly, and the instant mix and water curdle in my stomach.

"What?"

"I'm sorry, Elle. I just heard it from Hannah Grace's mom. I thought you might want to know."

I glance in the direction of Mrs. Whittaker who is dressed as Mrs. Claus and talking to several preschoolers anxiously waiting on the sleigh bells to announce Mr. Whittaker—Santa's—arrival.

"It's actually happening. She's really going through with it," I say more to myself than to Dawn.

Maybe deep down I hoped it was just a game. Even with the realtor sign mocking me in the front yard, I didn't want to believe it was true. I may have broken down once—okay, fine, three times—this week at seeing the sign sitting in the yard. A reminder that everything my parents built, everything I've dreamed of inheriting, is gone. Or will be very soon.

And every time I have driven by, the sleek blue rental car that sat in the driveway until recently is still gone.

I didn't want to believe that anything Trudy said was true. Including...even thinking his name made it hard to swallow around the lump in my throat.

Channing.

If he really had wanted more, wouldn't he have come after me when I left?

I stopped looking for him the second day I was at Merry's. I wasn't hiding from him. In a town the size of a postage stamp, it would be impossible to not find me. If he was looking.

I may be surrounded by people, but a pang of loneliness still punches me in the stomach to steal my breath.

Dawn's mouth is turned down, her eyes soft and kind as she reaches out a hand to squeeze my forearm.

"I'm sorry, Elle."

"It's okay. I'll be okay."

There's no other way for me to be, right? Distracting myself, I glance around as the clean-up crew finishes clearing the empty plates with leftover pancake crumbs and syrup and cups with rings of orange juice still visible in the bottom.

"Isn't Santa usually here by now?" I ask.

Dawn leans closer to me and lowers her voice.

"I saw Mr. Whittaker sidetracked by Fern, Fawn, and Merry a few minutes ago. There's no telling what the three of them had to talk to him about this morning."

I suck my lips into my mouth to try and keep my smile at bay. Those three women run pretty much everything in Mistletoe Creek. It's no wonder I can't say no to any of them —it seems like no one in town can.

And the three of them have the entire town fooled with their "bridge game." Until this last week when both Dawn and I had been invited into the inner circle. We had been sworn— and threatened—into secrecy. I didn't have the heart to tell them Dad had told me about their game years ago.

"Maybe I should go look for..."

The sound of jingle bells sewn into the sack of presents Mr. Whittaker brings every year interrupts, and the squeal of the kids is a symphony of chaos as they rush to their parents, ready to sit on Santa's lap and tell him what they'd like in just a few days.

I'm not sure when, in the last forty years that Breakfast with Santa had been a staple, that Santa had started bearing gifts, but each child in attendance always got something small and absolutely perfect for them. I still remember the year Santa—Mr. Whittaker's dad—had given me a book of illustrated fairy tales. The book is in a box in Merry's garage, waiting for my next step.

Is it any wonder this place is just as much a part of me as my eye color?

"Ho ho ho! Merry Christmas, Mistletoe Creek!" Mr. Whittaker waves and moves to the large chair set up at the front of the room.

"Merry Christmas, Santa," the entire room answers in chorus, adults included.

"It looks like everyone enjoyed breakfast again this year. Did you leave any for me?" he asks.

"Yes!" This time it's the kids yelling their response, and Mrs. Whittaker steps forward.

"Now, Santa, you can eat after you've visited with everyone. I've even wrapped a plate for you to take with you when you go to the North Pole."

"Very well, my dear, very well. So I suppose everyone here is ready to talk to Santa, hmm? Let me know those last-minute wishes?"

I wish Channing were here.

A year ago had I been asked what my wish was, it would have been for me to be able to renovate The Glass Slipper. To rebuild the inn into what my parents dreamed it could be.

When did Channing usurp that wish?

The moment you met him.

Maybe that's why his lack of communication hurts so bad. Because I've been falling for him since the first night. I assumed he had been too—but I guess I had been wrong.

The kids are bouncing excitedly and beginning to line up along the striped ribbon that marks the line.

"Elle Thompson, where are you?" Mr. Whittaker scans the room until he finds me. "Ahh, there you are. Come here. Santa has something for you."

"Me?" I point at myself and he nods.

Lifting a hand, he waves me forward as Dawn pushes from behind.

"There must be some mistake," I tell Mr. Whittaker when I'm close enough. "I'm not a kid, so I don't get a present."

"It doesn't matter how old or young you are, young lady. So long as you've been nice. I'm just responsible for handing out the presents." His eyes crinkle at the corner as he smiles behind the combination of fake and real beard.

"I'm sure what I want isn't in your bag, Santa."

Not unless it can magically fit a tall, dark, and handsome Prince Charming. Or an old converted Victorian house turned bed and breakfast.

"Well, let's see, shall we?"

Mrs. Whittaker hands her husband the red velvet bag of gifts, and he rummages inside to pull out a manila envelope ripped open on one side.

"It's addressed to you," he says and hands me the envelope.

"Tampering with the mail, Santa?"

But looking at the front I see the original address in the "to" area has been blacked out with permanent marker and my name is above it in loopy script.

Miss Elle Thompson.

A glance at the "from" area reveals nothing as it, too, has been blacked out. But the postmark is plain as day and marked *Nashville*.

"Open it," Fawn commands from next to Mrs. Whittaker.

Fern and Merry are in the front row, leaning forward in their seats until I'm afraid they'll fall forward.

Slowly, I open the flap and pull out the thin stack of papers.

Last Will and Testament of Mark Laird Thompson

I can't stop the tears that build and immediately fall as I

process the words. Lifting a hand, I swipe at them distractedly and continue to read.

I, Mark Laird Thompson, a resident of Mistletoe Creek, Tennessee, declare that this is my will. I revoke all wills and codicils I have previously made. In the manner of The Glass Slipper Bed & Breakfast, I give, devise, and bequeath an amount equal to sixty-five percent (65%) to my only daughter, Elle Marie Thompson.

Oh. My. God.

It was mine. The Glass Slipper—or at least the controlling portion of it—was mine. Not Trudy's. Not something to be sold and taken away.

Mine.

"What does it say, Elle?" Merry asks.

I lift my eyes to hers which are bright with tears.

"I-it's mine. Most of it."

She nods and I rush forward to wrap her in a hug.

"Miss Merry, I don't know how you found this—"

"Psssh. It wasn't hard. We knew what to do." She motions to the other two women. "We just didn't realize we had to. We really thought you knew and were trying to work with Trudy to run the inn. Or being kind and letting her and Alysa stay there with the other 35% willed to Trudy."

"D-does she know?"

Merry nods. "Your daddy told us he was clear with her from the beginning. The inn was always meant to be yours. It's what he and your mama wanted."

"Once we put two and two together, we—" Fawn begins.

"Santa," Mrs. Whittaker interrupts and shifts her eyes to the children.

"*Santa* got the copy of the will for you."

"Santa,"—Mrs. Whittaker turns to her husband—"maybe we ought to start talking to these sweet children. I know you're needed back home to prepare for Christmas Eve."

What do you think you're doing here?" He gestures toward the sitting room where the three business-suited guests stand and shuffle from foot to foot.

"What does it look like? I'm showing the house to Athenian Developments. They have some great ideas for the property—"

I almost feel bad for Trudy.

Is she really as out of touch as she seems? Or is it an Oscar-winning performance?

Regardless, the key word is almost.

"Mother, I've seen the will Mark filed with the state of Tennessee. Even if he had changed it, he would have had to file the changes with the state to make it valid. He didn't. You don't own enough of this place to sell anything. And if these developers were any good at their job, they would have pulled the information on this place before wasting a drive from Nashville to look at something you can't legally sell."

The three strangers make excuses before scurrying through the door to leave Channing, Trudy, and me alone.

"But Channing—" Trudy's lip trembles and her eyes well with tears.

Real or fake?

Is it sad I have to ask?

Probably.

Channing sighs and his body droops the longer he stands there. He's exhausted.

"Maybe you two should talk," I suggest.

"Yes, I think we should. Mother, why don't you go into the sitting room, and I'll be along in a minute?"

She doesn't say anything, but nods before walking into the sitting room, and it's just the two of us again.

"Elle—"

"Go. Go deal with her. We'll talk after."

He nods and turns in the direction of the sitting room,

but turns back and yanks me into his arms for a hug, his lips landing on mine in a bruising kiss.

"You'll be here?"

I nod.

"I will."

Because this is my home.

And I don't have to give it up. Now or ever again.

CHAPTER 16

Channing

etween the cramped ride in coach for most of my
flights and the conversation with Mother, I'm more
than ready for a reprieve when I open the sliding
doors to the sitting room an hour later.

"I'm going to go tell Alysa so we can pack," Mother
tells me.

"Probably a good idea. Your car should be here in about an
hour."

She reaches out, her arms lifted as if to hug me, but shies
away before she can make the connection. I close the distance
and loop my arms around her in a gentle hug.

"You're still my mother. And I love you. But like we talked
about, things have to change."

She nods into my shirt before stepping back. She's not the
woman of my childhood or the stranger I've lived with the last
few weeks, but somebody different. And I'm wondering if
maybe there is hope for her—and Alysa—yet.

Mother walks upstairs and down the hallway, and the
knock on Alysa's door echoes through the hall, but then everything is quiet again.

Reaching up, I lift a hand to the back of my neck. I'm exhausted, having only caught a little sleep at some point on the long day of flights as I made my way back. I managed to catch a few hours over the Pacific, but instead of waking up rested, I woke up with my head leaned awkwardly against the side of the plane and my knees scrunched after the person in front of me eliminated another tiny smidge of space between the coach seats.

Hayden would never be in charge of purchasing plane tickets again.

The remainder of the trip had been spent thinking about Elle, what I'd found out, and how to tell her she owned the majority of the inn.

Turns out, I didn't have to.

Witnessing her taking on Mother was a sight to behold. Even when I stepped in, it was more because I wanted to show her I had her back. That I chose her.

There's no sign of her in the entryway or in the office when I poke my head in the room. The light is on in the kitchen, and there's a bottle of honey near the electric tea kettle—I'm assuming it's her and not Alysa who used it.

I doubt she would have gone upstairs which leaves only one place left to check. Sure enough, I find her swinging lightly on the porch swing, bundled up in her coat, with a mug gripped between her fingers.

Two fresh brown hills in the yard are obvious, and I sit down next to her and gesture to the only remaining marks of the for sale sign.

"I'd have taken that down for you."

She shrugs.

"Easy enough to take care of."

"Did you throw the sign in the trash?"

I wouldn't be surprised if she did, and the mischievous

smile curving her lips lends itself to confirmation that she at least considered the idea.

"No. I was good. I stuck it in the garage."

"Garage?"

I've never seen any signs of one.

"It's behind the building. You've never been back there, huh?"

It had been on my list to finish cataloging the inn, but I hadn't made my way to the second back room and the outer buildings on the property.

"No."

She stands and reaches out a hand, and I grip it like the lifeline it is and let her lead me around the house. The lawn is more overgrown here, wilder than the front patch of grass.

"I don't get back here much," she says by way of apologizing.

"You have nothing to apologize for."

The house is bigger than it looks from the front, and I'm curious how big the back room is that is connected at the end of the hall but was locked the one time I tried the knob.

Elle produces a key and unlocks the door and we step in from the cold. It's one giant room with two bars in either corner—a room meant for entertaining.

She flips on the switch, and the lights flicker and gleam along polished wood despite the thin layer of dust coating everything.

"What is this place?"

"Mom and Dad used it for weddings or other celebrations. And the annual masquerade ball."

Her eyes meet mine for a split second before flitting away, but the way her breathing increases and the flush of her cheeks tells me the phrase *masquerade ball* has the same effect on her that it does on me.

"Masquerade ball?" I clear my throat to remove the husky quality.

"Mmm. Every year on New Year's Eve, Mom and Dad threw it. They liked the idea of a big party to celebrate with everyone, and it was their excuse to dress up as a prince and princess."

"Your dad was okay with that?"

She smiles the same angelic smile that drew me to her in a ballroom several hours away almost two months ago.

"He would have done anything to make her happy."

She lifts her fingers, and they find the ring on her necklace to toy with the white gold band.

"They loved each other." I take a step and close some of the distance between us, desperate to close the rest, but moving slow since I'm afraid to break the spell her words are weaving around us.

"They did."

"Do you still host the masquerade ball?"

"No. I wanted to, but since Trudy owns—"

"She doesn't. You own the majority stake."

"It's hard to wrap my brain around it."

"That this place is mostly yours?" I ask.

"Yeah."

She takes a step toward me, the two of us closing the distance in a choreographed dance of push and pull that's existed between us since the first night.

"I'm sorry," I tell her.

"Sorry? What do you have to be sorry for?"

"Mother knew all along the inn belonged to you."

"Why are you apologizing for her actions?"

"I—I don't know. It just feels like I need to. I have a car coming to pick up her and Alysa and take them to Nashville."

It hadn't taken Mother long to admit she wanted to move back to Nashville. She felt like she never fit in. Could never replace Mark's first wife and her presence that still existed in every piece of the place she unwillingly called home.

"Nashville?"

"They don't belong here. You deserve a fresh start. A chance to build this place into what you wanted all along."

"A fresh start. Will you be leaving with Trudy and Alysa for Nashville?"

She turns her back on me, pacing to the opposite end of the room, and I follow her.

"Is that what you want? You want me to go with them?"

Fuck, that's going to hurt. Walking away before had been an emergency. I don't know if I can walk away again.

"Elle?" I ask after several moments of silence stretch between us.

Maybe the silence is the only answer I need.

"It's not what I want." She turns back toward me, the tears in her eyes turning the warm brown into the color of molasses in the light filtering through the high windows.

"Fuck, sweets, don't cry. I'm here. I'm not going anywhere. Just don't cry." Reaching out a hand, I lift it to wipe an errant tear where it rolls down her cheek.

"Everything that's happened. It's like it's all hitting me at once." Her explanation is accompanied with more tears.

"This last week has been a whirlwind."

"No."

"No?"

"It's been more than this week. It's the reality that my mom and dad are gone. But that Dad did leave me this place. It was losing my home in the same day I lost you—"

"You didn't lose me, sweets."

"You left. Without saying goodbye, without looking for me, you just left."

The hurt is evident in her voice, and I would do anything I could to eliminate even the memory of it.

"That wasn't the plan."

"Trudy found me in your room, Channing. In your bed."

"I'm so fucking sorry about that. I was going to set the alarm, but instead I got distracted by a text from Hayden. We were going to lose the hotel lined up for our next project. I went downstairs to talk to him and ended up falling asleep in the office. That's why I didn't wake you up. I was asleep until after you left. By that point, I only had enough time to make it to the airport for my flight. And it's not like I had your phone number to contact you."

Her cheeks warm to a rosy shade of pink, and she drops her head.

"I didn't think of that."

"Neither did I, sweets. Nothing that morning was how I wanted things to happen. Including you taking on my mother on your own."

"I thought you left. Every time I drove by here this week, your car was gone. I figured what your mother said must have been right."

Dread curdles in my stomach to mix with anger. I can only imagine what Mother told her.

"Fuck. Do I even want to know?"

She grimaces.

"Well, like I said. She caught me in your room—"

"Why was she even in my room?"

She lifts one shoulder and lets it fall.

"We never talked about that. She told me I was a convenient distraction. That I was the help—"

"What the fuck?" I turn and take several steps away.

"She told me you were here to help her sell the inn."

"That's not why I was here." I retrace my steps until I'm directly in front of her.

Emotions play across her eyes—hurt, hope, anger—they all swirl in a mix and create an echoing response, and I want to yank her into my arms, but the move would negate the ability to let her see the truth for herself.

"It's not what you told me," she says and sinks her teeth into her bottom lip.

There's an urge to reach up, to release the pink flesh from her teeth, but I hold back.

"I came to spend the holidays with Mother and Alysa. But she did ask for my advice on whether to sell the inn or not," I say, and she sucks in a breath. Fuck, talk faster. "But that's not my final advice. I told Mother with some small renovations the inn could be profitable again. It definitely holds a niche that doesn't exist anywhere around here."

"If we book reservations," she mumbles.

"About that..."

"Okay?" Confusion carves a line between her brows.

"Alysa managed to use your passwords. She canceled all the existing reservations and listed the inn as unavailable during the month between Thanksgiving and Christmas. Seems she didn't like sharing her house with strangers."

"What a bi..." She catches herself before she can finish her sentence.

I chuckle.

"You can say it. I've told Mother she needs to be a better example. Alysa may be over the age of eighteen, but her maturity level, her entitlement, neither of those are going to make her a successful adult. And it may have been okay here, but in Nashville, she's in for a rude awakening."

"I think you're right."

"And I figured if I wanted to stand a chance to convince you to be with me I needed to get those two out of our hair."

"Be with you? Is that why you came back?"

"No, sweets. I came back because I can't stay away. I was in paradise and miserable because I forgot something when I left that morning."

"I'm sure it's—"

"Right here. You, Elle. I forgot my heart with you."

"You...what?"

Her eyes are bright with hope, but the line of confusion still wrinkles between her brows.

"I love you. Maybe the words are too simple or maybe not enough, but they are the bottom line. I started falling that night in Nashville and never stopped. Then I came here and saw the way you love this town, your connection to this place. I saw the real you, and I can't imagine loving anyone else the way I've fallen for you."

"But what about your job?"

Does she not feel the same way? Is that why she's throwing roadblocks up? Or is it fear?

"What about it?"

"You live out of a suitcase. One project to another."

"I may still travel occasionally, but I have no desire to leave here. Besides, I have a few projects closer to home that I think will keep me busy."

"Projects?" she asks.

"I want to help you turn this place into what you dreamed it could be."

The way her body melts at my words gives me courage to press on.

"And you," I tell her.

"Me? I'm a project?"

"Not you, sweets. But loving you is the best project I can think of. Showing you how special you are. Giving you what you deserve."

"Oh."

I can't fight the smile that curves my lips at her over-whelmed response. In her defense, I've just put a lot in her lap.

"It all depends on one thing," I tell her. Her eyes meet mine, and my future is visible in the warm depths. "You."

"Me?"

"The decision is yours. Whether you want me as much as I want you. If not—"

"I love you." She jumps toward me, looping her arms around my neck.

My hands settle on her hips and lift, pressing her close against my body that is completely on board with our reunion.

She gasps and muscle memory takes over. My mouth finds hers, my tongue tracing the seam of her lips until she opens for me. Everything around us disappears, leaving just the two of us in a room full of memories. My hands find her ass, and I squeeze her through the thick denim of her pants. She groans and grinds against my erection.

"Say it again," I command, breaking the kiss.

"I love you. I was scared to admit it since it happened so soon. But since the first night, I couldn't forget you. I couldn't resist when the universe dropped you back on my doorstep. Even though I tried."

"A valiant effort." I tease her and she smiles.

"I hated leaving the inn this week. But I hated even more when you weren't there. It was like a piece of me was—"

"Missing," I finish for her.

She nods.

"My heart. I gave it to you on Halloween without realizing it."

"I'll take care of it. I promise."

"I know."

I find her lips again and lose myself in her kiss until my phone vibrates in my pocket.

"Sweets?"

"Hmm?"

"As much as I love kissing you, I think the car service might be here."

I slowly lower her to her feet, but don't let her go just yet.

"Can we pick this back up in a few minutes?" I ask and bump my hips against hers. "Maybe somewhere a little more comfortable?"

Her eyes close on a low moan, and I nearly forget the need to get Mother and Alysa on the road. Luckily she steps back.

My dick presses against the zipper of my jeans painfully, and I palm myself through the denim and squeeze.

"We'll take the shortcut this time." She motions to the door, and I follow her to the solid oak door that leads into the inn. I cage her against it the same way I did at the hotel two months ago.

She drags her keys from her pocket, and my lips find the skin behind her ear.

"Are you going to tell me you never do this?" I ask.

She turns around and loops her arms around my neck to drag me back into a soul-connecting kiss.

"Only with you, Channing. Only with you."

Epilogue
CHANNING

"Alone at last," I say as Elle closes the door behind the last of our guests for the day.

She locks the deadbolt and turns around to lean against the door. A smear of dirt smudges her cheek, and her hair is wrapped in a bun that is more than messy at this point of the evening.

But she's never been more beautiful.

"It's been a busy day," she says.

The timbre of her voice is a mix of exhaustion and excitement, and I close the distance to pull her into my arms.

"I think we must have had everyone in the town here at one point or another."

They had started shortly after we woke up and had kept coming with carloads full of people and cleaning supplies.

"Are you still okay with us hosting the masquerade ball here again?" She leans her chin against my chest and I tighten my arms around her.

"I wouldn't have suggested it if I wasn't. It was a staple of the holidays in this town for years. I want it to be again. Plus, it reminds me of our first night together."

Her pupils dilate, and her tongue peeks out to slick against her lips. My dick hardens in a heady rush.

"Me too." Her voice has a husky quality to it as she crushes her breasts against my chest.

Fuck, I want to kiss her. I want to carry her into the sitting room and ravish her under the Christmas tree we put up yesterday after I dug it out of a storage shed behind the house.

But I have plans. And kissing her right now fucks those plans to hell in a hand basket.

"I'm sorry I couldn't help," I say and drop a kiss to the end of her nose before taking a step back and allowing the cool air to rush between us and lower the temperature back down to tolerable levels.

Her brows furrow as she studies me for several moments until they smooth once more.

"You were helping. I feel like I got the easy job."

"Cleaning the back room couldn't have been easy." I lift my fingers and swipe at the smudge of dirt on her cheek until it's gone.

"You reached out to all the canceled reservations and explained what happened. You also shifted the website to the automated platform I had begged Dad to do for years before he passed."

"And The Glass Slipper is fully booked beginning February 2."

"February?"

"I didn't think the guests would appreciate the noise of the renovations during construction. The crew shows up here January 3rd."

Her eyes become luminescent with unshed tears.

"Channing, I love that you love this inn like I do. But there's no money saved—"

I wave away her comment.

"The inn needs to make money. It's what I know how to do. Once it's back in the black, you can pay me back then."

And I'll put the money aside for something else for the inn or for her. I don't need the money, and for years, Mother and Alysa treated this place as a contemptible ATM. It was perfectly fine to spend the money when neither of them worked for it.

"But what about the Fiji hotel? Doesn't Hayden need your help?"

I shake my head.

"Hayden can handle Fiji now that it's back on track. I want to be here. I want to do this with you."

The thought of leaving here—leaving her—again is unacceptable.

"Oh."

"Is that okay?" I ask.

She nods.

"Yes."

"So we have a deal?"

"It's a deal."

She reaches out her hand to shake on it, and I wrap mine with hers and haul her back into my arms.

"How about we kiss on it instead of shake hands?"

She lifts to her tiptoes, and her mouth brushes mine lazily in a teasing caress. Lifting my hand to her hair, I wrap her ponytail in my fist and tug her head where I want it so I can seal my lips to hers. My tongue presses against her lips and she gasps, allowing me in to dance with hers.

Her fingers find my biceps, the tiny pinpricks of her nails enough of a reality check that I break the kiss when what I really want is to keep it going until I'm buried inside her.

"It's Christmas Eve, sweets," I tell her.

She bounces in my arms, her excitement infectious.

"I know."

"What was your tradition growing up, present wise?"

"One present Christmas Eve, the next day were the rest and presents from Mom and Dad. And every year on Christmas Eve I opened a new pair of Christmas pajamas and a Christmas movie we watched until it was time for me to go to bed. You?"

"I know it's hard to believe this, but growing up, my mom was a different type of person. Our traditions were pretty similar. Except for the Christmas PJs part."

"Really?"

I nod, and memories of Christmas Eves spent with Mother and Dad and then Alysa when she came along come to mind. The handmade ornaments treated with the preciousness of the most expensive ornament. I'll have to ask Mother what happened to those.

"Channing?"

Her tone of voice suggests it's not the first time she's said my name.

"I'm sorry, what?"

"Is that what you want to do? Keep that tradition?"

Her question creates a warm, fuzzy sensation in my body.

"What do you think?"

"I like that idea. There's just one problem."

"What's that?" I ask.

"There's nothing under the tree. It's not like either of us has had time to go anywhere."

"Are you sure about that?" I lift an eyebrow and she laughs.

"Yes, we've both been too busy. With last-minute plans for the masquerade ball and you trying to do all things electronic and financial related, when would we have had time to go anywhere?"

"What if Santa came?"

"Santa?"

I shrug and pull her into the sitting room where the tree and the fireplace are the only lights in the room. I've brought a bottle of champagne in a chiller bucket and a platter full of snacks I created from the odds and ends in the refrigerator.

The quick gasp of breath when she takes it all in is the only reward I need.

"When did you do this?"

"Today after I finished up in the office. Have a seat."

I motion to the plush blanket in front of the fireplace next to the tree and wait for her to lower herself to it before pouring her a glass of champagne.

I pour one for myself, and she holds it while I situate myself on the blanket with her.

"Has anyone told you you're a bit of a romantic?"

"Only for you, sweets."

She leans over and hovers her lips over mine and brushes against them with her words.

"I love you."

"I love you too."

She kisses me like we've been kissing for years instead of weeks. The comfortable kind of kiss that happens between soulmates. It's a steady burn instead of flash until I pull back.

"Sweets."

"Hmm?"

"There's something under the tree. I believe it has your name on it."

Her eyes pop open and she follows my gaze to the small box loosely wrapped under the tree.

"You were telling the truth?"

"Why would I lie?"

"Good point," she says.

"Don't you want to open it?" I ask her.

Once she nods, I reach under the tree and pull the box free to rest it in front of her.

"What is it?"

"Open it and find out," I tell her.

With slow movements, she pulls the thread on the ribbon, opening the paper with a precision I can't understand. It makes my palms itch to rip it open for her. But I wait.

Finally, she lifts the lid on the box where an antique iron key is tied to a sheaf of papers with a red satin bow.

"What's this?" She lifts her gaze to mine.

"The papers are a legal document I had my attorney draw up. I bought Mother's thirty-five percent from her. But it was for you. These documents gift you the inn in its entirety. It's yours, Elle. It was always meant to be yours."

"Channing." Tears build and spill over to run unchecked down her face.

Reaching over, I wipe them away with my thumbs.

"A-and the key?"

A corner of my lips twitch with a smile.

"I'm probably a bit of a dork. It is a symbol."

"A symbol of what?"

"A key to my heart. I love you, sweets. And I want to stay here with you. Help you make your dream for this inn—whatever dream you come up with—come true."

"I love you too."

"Does that mean I can stay?"

"Of course!" She leans forward, nearly into my arms when she stops, eyes widening almost comically.

"What's the matter?"

"I...your present is upstairs. I'll be right back."

She rushes from the room, and while I wait, I pick up the wrapping paper and ball it up to toss it into the trash later.

I'm still waiting, and I'm half tempted to go find Elle when she reappears in the doorway.

"Did you forget something?"

"No."

The Cheshire cat smile on her face fills me with curiosity, a mix of desire and mischief.

Fuck, I love this woman.

"Your hands are empty," I tell her.

She nods and lowers herself to sit in front of me.

"Your present is right here."

She grips the bottom of her red pajama shirt and whips it off to reveal red silk material that hugs her breasts with mouth-watering precision. Her nipples tighten and push against the fabric and beg for my touch.

"Fuck, Elle."

The clock in the hall strikes midnight while I catalog every fold of the silk against her skin.

"Merry Christmas, Channing."

"Merry Christmas, sweets."

It's the last thing I say as I push forward, my lips capturing hers.

I'm home.

AND THEY LIVED HAPPILY EVER AFTER.
THE END.

Thank you so much for reading!

LOVE THE IDYLLIC SMALL TOWN OF MISTLETOE CREEK? Come back for a visit with Cole, a former MMC hometown hero, and his second chance, forced proximity romantic suspense, BODYGUARD FOR THE BEAUTY QUEEN. Keep reading for a sneak peek!

BEFORE YOU GO! Want to attend the masquerade ball? Turn the page to see how Channing and Elle's New Year's Eve turns out...

Bonus Epilogue

ELLE

I still have a thousand and one things to do tonight, but Merry called me thirty minutes ago, and I now find myself on her front porch, knocking on her door.

The solid wood door swings open on a burst of energy, and I step back with the fear of being run over.

"You're here! You're here! Come in!" Merry pushes open the screen door and drags me into the house.

"Miss Merry, you said this was an emergency."

I had expected to come over and find her hurt. Or her old dachshund, Bernie, needing help. Instead he prances around my heels like a puppy while Merry tugs me the rest of the way into her sewing room.

"Well, I may have fibbed."

No kidding.

"Miss Merry, we've talked about these types of emergencies before."

Like when she burst into my room at five in the morning during the week I stayed here because I had to wake up to watch an article on the news about Mistletoe Creek when it was a thirty-second overview of our Christmas activities.

"This is important, Elle."

Staying mad at Merry—or Fawn or Fern—is an impossible feat. They may be bossy, eccentric, and opinionated, but they are all an integral thread to the colorful blanket that makes up my hometown.

"Okay, Miss Merry, tell me what's going on." I relax my stance and try to forget the daunting to-do list that waits for me back at the inn.

Merry turns to the closet in the room and pulls out a swath of periwinkle blue chiffon under a gauzy lace overlay.

"What's that? It's so pretty." I reach out a hand before I can change my mind and drag my fingertip along the smooth fabric.

"It's for you."

"Me?"

She nods.

"I've held on to this dress since the year your Mama passed."

"The first year we didn't host the ball."

Merry nods, her eyes slanted down and filled with empathy.

Mom had gotten diagnosed in October, and even though she tried to convince Dad and me to hold the ball—it was always her favorite event of the season—that year she was too sick to host it. And by the next year after she had passed, neither of us had the heart for it.

"Your Mama reached out to me that year. She wanted me to create a dress for her. I reminded her that I had retired years ago, but she didn't care. All she knew is she wanted a dress. One that reminded her of her favorite princess."

"Cinderella."

Merry smiles, a barely there tip of her lips as she continues her story.

"That's right. I loved the idea, so I kept working on the dress even after we found out about..."

The cancer.

I don't say it out loud and neither does she, but the word is a tangible thing in the room with us.

"You've had it all these years?"

Merry nods.

"I was waiting for the next ball. I kept thinking maybe they'd come back either from your dad or someone else would decide to host it. And after a few years, I was sure it had disappeared. But now you and your young man—"

"Channing."

"Yes, I know," she huffs.

I lift my hand to hide my smile.

"You and *Channing*. You've brought it back."

"It was his idea."

She nods, expecting my answer.

"I think you should wear this tonight." She lifts the dress and allows it to catch the light.

I had planned to wear the same dress I did in Nashville since I haven't had the chance to go buy anything else.

"What if it doesn't fit?"

Her expression is a mix of outrage in her upturned lip and confidence in the easy set of her eyes.

Reaching over, she lifts up a pin cushion that reminds me more of a porcupine.

"Who do you think you're talking to?" she asks with an arch of her brow. "Let's get to work."

Do you remember how we met? I'll meet you at the ball. Love, Charming

Heat builds in my core as I read Channing's note.

Charming, huh?

We can definitely recreate that night. Only without me running the next morning.

"I'm here! I'm here!" Posey bursts in through the door of the bed and breakfast.

I fold the note and tuck it into my pocket.

"What's that?"

"Nothing. Will there ever be a day you're on time?" I tease and change the subject, not willing to share my sexy fantasy with her.

"I'm sorry...Dave and I were fighting. And then making up." She winks like I don't catch the meaning.

"Dave as in your boss, Dave?" I ask.

"Yeah."

"I thought you didn't like him. You definitely complain about him enough."

"He's a dick at work." She shrugs like it's enough of an explanation.

Newsflash. It's not.

"Posey!"

"I know."

"I thought you said he was married?"

"They're getting a divorce."

Inhaling a deep breath, I count to three before exhaling. I'm the last person who will ever judge her for anything. She's my best friend. Not to mention she showed up last minute to support Channing and me and the ball tonight.

Just the thought of his name brings to mind his note and increases the urgency I have to go find him.

"Okay," I tell her.

"Okay?"

She's locked in place, braced for something else, and her entire body deflates with the one word.

"If he makes you happy, I'm happy."

"He does."

"So let's go get ready, and you can tell me more about the non-dick version of him."

She spends the entire time we do hair and makeup trying to convince someone about him. I'm just not sure if it's her or me. She says she's happy, but something doesn't sit right. It may be the fact that he's married—going through a divorce or not. It may be because Posey never had anything nice to say about him before now. Or that she didn't tell me sooner.

Is it because he's her boss?

You told her about Channing and he's your stepbrother.

We've told each other everything since we were in kindergarten. So why start keeping secrets now?

"Ready?" I turn from the mirror where I've been applying my lipstick.

"Yep." Her phone starts to ring as she says it, and she glances down at the screen. "Dave. Hi, honey."

"Do you want me to wait?" I ask.

She waves a hand toward the door.

"No, I'll come find you in a bit. No, I was talking to Elle. No. She's my best friend. Yeah, we were talking about—"

She stops and listens to him before trying to speak again.

"But—"

Again, her silence and then she walks out of the room. The sliding doors on the sitting room open and shut with an echo, and I'm left alone in my bedroom at the top of the stairs.

"What the hell was that?" I ask my reflection.

My phone vibrates and I glance down.

CHANNING

coming soon?

I hope so. But I may need your help.

Several seconds tick by as I wait for the dots to stop dancing with his response.

> Thanks. I nearly sprayed my drink all over Merry, Fern, and Fawn.

> sorry!

> I'll rephrase. When can I see you?

After one last glance in the mirror, I head downstairs and leave my phone on our dresser.

I use the back entrance from the house into the event space and sneak to the edge of the room to scan it for signs of Channing.

The room itself is dotted with white twinkle lights and silver ornaments to reflect the light in different directions. The wood along the bar and on the floor is polished to a gleam, and the windows sparkle and pick up the lights throughout the space.

It's not exactly how I remember it.

It's better. Dawn and Phillip are dancing in one part of the room, oblivious to anyone or anything around them. Fern, Fawn, and Merry are gathered around a table deep in conversation. Probably on who they can set up together next.

But no sign of—

"I've been looking for you forever, Cinderella."

Channing.

The deep voice that echoed those words over two months ago murmurs in my ear, his lips brushing the sensitive skin as he speaks.

A shiver works its way down my spine, and goose bumps ripple just like they did then.

I whirl around, the full skirt twirling with me to take him in.

The same dark mask is in place, and a five o'clock shadow darkens his cheeks. His brown eyes study me from the top of my head to the bottom of my dress, and the heat in his gaze sets a fire along every nerve ending.

"Does your line work on a lot of women?" I ask. My voice is huskier than it was, and my shallow breaths attract his attention to my chest for several moments.

"You tell me. I've never used it before. This is new." His last words catapult me into the present.

He lifts his hand, and his thumb and forefinger play with a small ribbon at my shoulder.

Each shoulder has a small ribbon where the strap flows to the dress. The deep v on my chest is softened by the lacy overlay that covers the whole thing, and the full skirt is almost like a ball gown but not quite as fluffy.

It's Cinderella. It's Mom. And it's perfect.

I nod.

"Merry gave it to me this morning. It was the last dress she ever made for my mom."

It's like she's here. She and Dad. Sitting with their friends to visit. Out on the dance floor swaying together.

"Merry made that?"

"Yeah. She used to have a custom shop close to Mistletoe Café."

"It's beautiful. And you, sweets, are stunning."

I've curled my hair and pulled half of it up off my face. My eye makeup is light behind the replacement mask I had to order since the original was left behind in the hotel room with Channing, and my lips are darker, a bold red that I hope captures his attention until he kisses it off.

"You told me that before," I remind him.

"It was as true then as it is now. Maybe more so." He steps forward and brushes a light kiss along my cheek.

The heat of him wraps me in a fog of sandalwood and

lavender and I suck in a breath. His hand splays on the fabric that covers my stomach while his fingertips brush the underside of my breasts.

"Channing," I moan softly.

"Not tonight. Remember? Charming."

And he is. The entire night he's by my side, talking to the people who came to support us until he tugs me onto the dance floor and lets the rest of the world float away. He's there at midnight when the clock ticks into a new year and at the end of the night when it's just the two of us at our bedroom door.

"I never do this," I whisper into the door.

Channing's hands come up and cup my breasts, squeezing through the fabric, and my core pulses with need. His lips trail hot, open-mouthed kisses along my neck and across my shoulder.

Mewling, I press against him, wanting more.

"Only with me, sweets."

I reach up and back, threading my fingers through his hair and pushing my breasts farther against his hands.

"I've warned you about those hands, Cinderella."

"Yes, you did."

"Maybe I should do something about them," he growls and walks us into our room.

"Maybe you should." My challenge ends on a gasp as he sweeps me off my feet.

I yank his mask off followed by mine and toss them into the corner.

"This is different," he says.

"This is forever," I tell him just before his lips claim mine.

NOT QUITE READY TO LEAVE MISTLETOE CREEK?
Neither am I.
What is Christmas like in this idyllic small town a year later?
TURN THE PAGE to find out...

Bonus Epilogue 2

ELLE

1 YEAR LATER

"Are you sure you don't want to sit down?" I ask Dawn as we man the hot chocolate table at Breakfast with Santa.

She pushes one hand into her back while the other rubs at her *very* swollen stomach.

"I'm fine." She tries to smile but the twist to her lips is more grimace than happiness. "Just a few more days. Besides, if I sit down, I'm not sure I'll want to stand up when it's time to go home."

"I can't believe your baby is due on Christmas," I tell her before I grab a folding chair from nearby and put it close to her.

I don't have to say anything again and she sits with a groan.

"We do live in a town that's crazy about Christmas. I can't sit like this for long."

"Why not?"

"At nine months pregnant, doing anything for too long hurts."

"Isn't Mr.–er–Claus here by now?" I glance around the room, and the kids are all finished with breakfast and anxiously awaiting the man of the hour.

Dawn shrugs. "He was late last year."

"I hope it doesn't become a habit. Otherwise maybe we ought to adjust the time if he needs a little more to get ready."

"He got sidetracked by Fern, Fawn, and Merry last year."

"Those three are accounted for." I point to the table right in front of Santa's chair.

"I'm sure he'll be here any minute."

As if on cue, the sleigh bells jingle in the hallway.

Where's Channing? He got a phone call from Hayden ten minutes ago and disappeared. I want him to see this since he missed it last year.

"Ho ho ho! Merry Christmas!" Mr. Whittaker booms as he enters the room with his red velvet bag.

There's a chorus of responses to his greeting.

"It's Santa!"

"Mom!"

"Merry Christmas, Santa!"

Mrs. Whittaker moves forward, greeting her husband and helping with his bag. Based on the expression on her face, there may also be a lecture going on only he can hear. But by the time he settles in his chair, both of them are smiling like nothing happened.

"Has everyone been good little boys and girls this year?" he asks the children standing in line next to him.

"Yes!" they shout.

"I can't wait for my baby to experience this." Both of Dawn's hands now cradle her stomach.

"He or she is going to love it. We all have."

Dawn and Phillip have shared they don't want to know ahead of time what they're having which is driving everyone in town nuts with the baby pool Fern put together. For a small fee, anyone can guess gender, birth date, weight, and name. Once the baby is born, the plan is to donate the pot to Dawn and Phillip.

"Have you seen Channing?" I ask.

Dawn shakes her head. "Not since he took that phone call."

"Maybe I—"

"Elle? Elle Thompson?"

Santa searches the room until his eyes land on mine. It doesn't help that half the town is also pointing to me.

"Not again. She was first last year and she's not even a kid." The little voice rings out only to be shushed by a parent.

"What's going on?" I turn to Dawn.

She shakes her head with a shrug. "No idea. Better go find out."

With a sigh, I step out from behind the table and make my way to the stage.

"We've got to stop meeting like this, Santa."

His chuckle is so authentic it fills me with a warmth and belief I haven't had since I was a young girl.

"I told you last year, young lady. I'm just the delivery man."

He hands me a small box he pulls from his pocket. It's smaller than any box I've seen, the miniature wrapping reminding me of a dollhouse I saw as a childhood. Maybe it belongs in one of the gingerbread houses from this year.

"What is it?"

"I'd like to know too," he says and gestures for me to open it.

It takes me a moment to figure out how it pops open, but once it does, my breath catches in my throat. Nestled inside the plush fabric is a white gold band with round diamonds flanking a center-cut diamond that sparkles from its surrounding partners.

"What is it? What'd she get?" another little voice asks.

I lift my eyes from the ring to the man who delivered it. He nods behind me, and I turn to find Channing on one knee.

"Channing."

"Elle Marie Thompson, I figured this was the perfect place to tell you how much I love you. I wasn't looking for anything or anyone like you just over a year ago. And now I can't imagine a day without you. I asked Santa for his help to give you that, but it's me asking you this question. To share your forever with me. To be mine. I asked Fern, Fawn, and Merry for their blessing—"

"Which we gave you," Fawn interrupts.

Channing and I smile simultaneously. I'll never convince them to stop matchmaking after this.

Do you care?

"What do you say, sweets? Will you marry me?"

I'm nodding before I can get the word to come out through the happy tears making their way down my face.

"Yes, yes, I'll marry you."

Channing stands, tugging me to him and finding my lips with his.

"Ewww, they're kissing."

"Shhh."

The world doesn't quite fade away with the commentary, but my eyes are only on him—on my fiancé—when we finally break the kiss.

"I love you," he says and gently takes the ring out of the box to slide it on my finger.

"I love you too."

He's my forever. And it can't end any better than happily ever after.

Bodyguard for the Beauty Queen

COLE

7 YEARS AGO

"What's the matter, Honey Girl?" I glance away from the windshield to spy my girlfriend curled up on the opposite side of the truck seat, clutching the door handle and looking like third runner-up in the Miss Mistletoe Creek County Fair Pageant.

But even me using a nickname for her that ordinarily makes her smile only creates a sigh.

Fuck.

I flip on the radio, tuning in to our favorite station as we wind the back roads through the foothills of the Smokies that surround our hometown of Mistletoe Creek, Tennessee. The reception is spotty the farther up we drive, but it fills the silence as I rack my brain and try to figure out how to make our last night together a happy memory rather than a sad one.

I'm going to need that memory to keep me going until I can see her again. Hopefully ten weeks from now when I'm finishing up basic. That's if she can make it out to South Carolina for my graduation.

She's still waiting on the information on when her freshmen move-in date is. I'm so fucking proud of my girl for getting into Vanderbilt.

"I'm fine," she says.

But the normal lyrical cadence to her voice is flat. Robotic.

"Sweetheart, it's been a long time since you weren't snuggled against my side. And the last time you were this quiet was the time you lost your voice at the football game we won against Devil Falls."

I find the turn that's little more than a gap between two of the trees. The path is clear, but only barely fits my old truck. Between the bumps and the trees I've skimmed with my fingers when my window is down, I can't watch for her response.

The trees finally spread out more until they're in my rearview and all that's left in front of us is a vista of Mistletoe Creek. The high school is on the edge of town, quiet now that school is out for the summer, and the rest of the little town nestles around it. It's idyllic and it's charming, but it's too small for what I want in my life. I've grown up here, but I'm not willing to just settle down and be a Volunteer before coming back to work in Dad's distillery. That plan might make sense for Justin and Jared, but I am not like my older brothers.

It's what makes the military so exciting—because it wasn't planned out for me.

I put the truck in park and reach for Hannah Grace's hand to tug her toward me.

"Han."

"Don't."

Fuck. Her voice is thick with tears, and proof of one drops on my hands.

"Sweetheart."

I pull her against my chest, rubbing my hand along her back while she sobs into the cotton of my T-shirt.

The scent of her citrus shampoo tickles my nose, and I take a deep breath.

"It's our last night together, baby. I don't want you to cry."

I don't want this memory.

Already the guilt is enough to have me second-guessing my choice.

"I don't want you to go," she mumbles, the words hard to understand through the tears and hiccuping breaths.

"I know." I drop my lips to her hair and keep the steady rhythm of my hand on her back.

She leans up, those cornflower-blue eyes shiny with tears.

"It didn't feel real before, Cole. I want this to be a dream. To wake up tomorrow and not have to say goodbye." Her lower lip trembles, and she sinks her teeth into it to stop the vibration.

I lift my hand and glide my thumb along the swollen flesh.

"It's not forever," I tell her.

More tears slide under my palm that rests against her cheek.

"I can call you...and write. And it's only ten weeks until graduation."

"It's not the same. I've seen you every day for as long as I can remember. I won't be able to do this"—she runs her hands up my chest— "when you're four hours away."

I try to ignore my body's natural reaction to her touch, but my dick jumps. And since she's almost on top of me, I can't hide it.

"Fuck, Hannah Grace, I'm sorry. I didn't bring you up here for this." I groan and lean my head back against the seat.

Even though *this* is something I've thought about since I hit puberty.

"I know. You've never..."

"No."

I respected Hannah Grace too much to push her to do something she wasn't ready for. I respected my own mama's hand upside the back of my head too. I didn't need any other reason to make her want to use it. Between five kids, she has plenty of her own reasons.

Her expression shifts, the tears only salty trails on her cheeks, while mischief tilts her lips.

"What's that look, Hannah Grace Whittaker?"

It's one that's never boded well for me.

In fact it normally results in one or both of us getting grounded.

It's not like Mom can ground me, since I'm leaving tomorrow morning.

It's an accurate statement, but I'm still hesitant to go along with anything involved in that particular expression on Hannah's face.

The last time had resulted in us launching over a thousand bouncy balls in the high school's auditorium during the county's beauty pageant that Hannah hadn't wanted to participate in. Turns out, it didn't stop the pageant. However, it did end up getting back to both our mamas.

Being grounded and voluntold into helping with the high school's locker clean-out day was a consequence I never wanted to live again. Several lockers hadn't been cleaned out all year—and the lunch bag/science experiments inside had proven it.

"Why did you bring me up here?"

"This is our spot, sweetheart. I couldn't imagine our last date happening anywhere else. My favorite view in this world is this view with you in it."

Reaching forward, I grab my phone off the dash and shake it toward her.

"Come with me," I tell her and open my door.

"No pictures. I'm a mess. I'm all splotchy." She tries to

stay in the car, but our connected hands make it easy to tug her out.

"You're not splotchy; you'll always be beautiful to me," I murmur and brush a kiss on the tip of her nose.

Her hands come up and rest against my biceps, her fingers skimming the underside of my arms and coming close to my ticklish spot.

I shy away.

"No, you don't."

"It pays to have known you forever," she tells me and sneaks past my defenses to run her fingers up my side.

I giggle and clear my throat as I wrap my arms around her and hold her to my chest with her hands trapped between us.

"Gotcha," I say.

She moves to her tiptoes and puckers her lips in my direction, and I oblige by covering her mouth with mine.

"Would you please take a picture with me?" My lips tease hers with my question. "I want to have one with me that's recent. That's us. Not made-up for prom. But the real us."

"How do you always know what to say that makes me want to say yes?"

Her question is innocent enough, but I hope there's more truth to it since I have another question to ask her. One more important than to take a picture with me.

I position us so that she's still wrapped in one arm, the vista behind us, and lift the camera to capture one selfie of the two of us smiling.

"How about one with a kiss?" she suggests.

"Hannah Grace!" I hold my phone against my chest, pretending an affront that the older generation in our town has down pat.

Something I will never say to the leaders of that generation —Fern, Fawn, and Merry. Although deep down, I think they enjoy watching young couples in love.

"Stop pretending like you don't want to kiss me, Cole Strickland." She smacks my chest playfully.

I oblige her request for a kiss and lift my camera at just the right time to capture the two of us locked together. I manage to separate us before my hormones take over then pocket my phone.

My fingers brush the velvet box in my pocket, and I suck in a deep breath as Hannah turns in my arms to focus on the view at our feet.

I clear my throat again, swallowing the lump of nerves that wants to take up residence on my vocal cords.

"I'm going to miss you, sweetheart," I whisper.

She rotates in my arms and squeezes her arms around me.

"I'm going to miss you too."

"I love you."

It's not the first time I've said the words, but this is the moment when they take on the most meaning they've ever had.

"I love you," she murmurs and presses her lips against my heart.

"Hannah Grace, I've loved you for forever, and I'm going to love you for the rest of my life. Maybe even longer."

"Cole?" She looks up, her brows furrowed as she studies my expression.

I take advantage and drop my lips to hers again. She's where I find my strength and my peace. And I doubt she even realizes it.

"I've known I was going to marry you from the time I was ten years old. You walked into the community center Christmas dance in that red party dress with white lace—the one you told me you hated—and all I could think about was how soft it looked. And how nice you were to wear it because your mama wanted you to match the dress she had."

"What are you saying, Cole?"

"I won't ask you to marry me now, Hannah Grace. Partly because I haven't talked to your daddy for his permission, but mostly because I want to see you finish school, sweetheart. I'm so fucking proud of you for getting into Vanderbilt. And I refuse to let you give that up to follow me. You're going to be something, baby. And I'm going to be cheering you on. But until then, I won't ask you the question I really want and instead, I want to make you a promise. Someday, Hannah Grace, someday I'm going to ask you to marry me. With your daddy's blessing and when we're ready. Nothing is going to stop me." I pull the box from my pocket and flip up the lid. "It's not a ring, not yet. I want you to have one—the one you deserve—but I also wanted you to have something that sealed my promise."

I lift out the chain where a key rests next to a small heart with the initials C and H engraved in it.

"What I'm asking is if you'll accept my promise? If you'll let me love you forever and wait for me, for us, for the right time. To someday be my wife."

She nods furiously, throwing her arms around me as soon as I'm done with the speech I've rehearsed a thousand times.

"Yes!"

My arms tighten around her and I hold her to me, burying my head in her neck and breathing in her sweet citrus scent.

She said yes.

Her lips find mine, and she bounces in my arms until we break the kiss with a laugh.

"Put it on me, please?"

She spins again, and I lift the necklace over her head and wait for her to move her hair out of the way.

"There." Closing the clasp, I kiss the back of her neck and relish the shiver that works its way down her spine.

"Cold, sweetheart?" I ask, already knowing that even in the mountains, our June weather is hard to be cold in.

"Can we get back in the truck?" Her question catches me off guard.

"Sure. Sorry. I didn't think. It is colder up here..." I boost her into the truck and climb in behind her.

The door snicks shut and she straddles me, her mouth claiming mine while her hands grip the hem of my T-shirt and tug. My dick hardens in a rush, pushing against the zipper of my shorts.

"Whoa, whoa, whoa, what's all this?" I ask, pulling away and holding her at arm's length when she appears ready to dive back in again.

"I want to, Cole. I—"

"I didn't make my promise for anything like this from you, Hannah Grace. We can wait."

"*I* can't wait. I want you. Right now."

She grinds her pelvis against my dick, and I can't hold back the moan that works its way out of my throat. Every part of my self-control is focused on being a gentleman even though she's telling me that's not what she wants.

Her lips find the pulse point in my neck and her tongue laves the spot, pleasure overwhelming every other conscious thought.

"Please. We just have tonight."

Apparently done fighting my shirt, she sits up and lifts hers over her head, displaying a perfect pair of tits clad in a light-pink lace bra.

I squeeze my eyes shut and fist my hands into the cotton of her shorts. She wiggles some more before grabbing my hands and lifting them to her now bare chest, and my eyes fly open to find my traitorous palms grazing the soft skin of her breasts, her nipples poking into the center of my palms.

"*Please.*"

Any chance I had of fighting against her temptation evaporates. With more strength than I think I have, I lift one hand

and cup her nape to bring her lips back to mine and give in to the fire that burns us both until all that's left is the two of us... no longer two, but one.

What happens after Cole leaves Mistletoe Creek and Hannah Grace? You can binge his second chance, forced proximity happily ever after, BODYGUARD FOR THE BEAUTY QUEEN, on KU!

Playlist

The playlist for *Midnight in Mistletoe* is short, sweet, and packs a punch! Songs like "Maroon" by Taylor Swift, "This is Me" by Keala Seattle, & "From the Ashes" by Illenium ft. Skylar Grey are all Elle. Meanwhile "Fallin' All in You" by Shawn Mendes and Andrew Belle's "Pieces of You" really tell the story of Channing's love for his princess.

Want to listen to the music inspired by Channing and Elle's love story? Check out the playlist on Spotify by searching for the "Midnight in Mistletoe" playlist or scan the QR code.

You can both the playlist and the bonus tracks on my website:

https://www.breannalynnau thor.com

Acknowledgments

To you. Yes, you. The one who just read Channing and Elle's happily ever after! Thank you for taking the chance on the two of them. I always wanted to write a fairytale retelling and I hope you enjoyed reading *Midnight in Mistletoe* as much I enjoyed writing it!

For my family—thank you for being excited for me, for sharing my books, and for supporting me! I love you!

For the fellow ladies of Mistletoe Creek—it's been a wild ride, but I've had so much fun this year!

Claire and Alina—Special shout out to the two of you because you're you. Whether I'm writing or not, you love me! You also kick my butt when I should be writing. Love you both!

For Ann R and Ann S—Thank you for being encouraging, for being patient, and for turning this book around as fast as you did!

This journey continues to be a wild ride and I can't imagine taking it without any of you!

XOXO,
    Breanna

Also by Breanna Lynn

HEART BEATS SERIES

Written in the Beat

In The Beat of the Moment

Keeping the Beat

Betting on the Beat

Embracing the Beat

Falling for the Beat

SAFE HAVEN SECURITY

Soldier for the Starling

Bodyguard for the Beauty Queen

Detective for the Debutante

STAND ALONE NOVELLAS

Rockin' Around the Christmas Tree

Midnight in Mistletoe

Hating Mr. Write

One Weekend in Vegas

About the Author

Breanna Lynn lives in Colorado with her two sets of twins (affectionately referred to as the Twinx), her boyfriend, his son, their two dogs, and three cats. A classy connoisseur of all things coffee, Breanna spends her free time keeping the Twinx from taking over the world. When not coordinating chaos, Breanna can be found binge reading, listening to music, or watching rom-coms with a giant bowl of popcorn.

Want to follow Breanna? Scan the QR code for all the ways to stay caught up!